IN A DRY SEASON

When the village of Hobb's End in Yorkshire was submerged beneath a reservoir in the 1950s, evidence of a terrible death was concealed.

Forty years on, when the heat of summer exposes the bones of a young woman in the dry valley bed, the secrets of the past re-emerge.
DCI Banks, called in to investigate, finds himself piecing together clues to a wartime drama of sexual rivalry and thwarted passion.

IN A DRY SEASON

SELECT EDITIONS

This condensation has been created by The Reader's Digest Association Limited by special arrangement with Macmillan Publishers Ltd.

The Reader's Digest Association Limited,
11 Westferry Circus, Canary Wharf, London E14 4HE.

www.readersdigest.co.uk
ISBN 0 276 42553 7

Printed and bound by GGP Media, Pössneck, Germany

Peter Robinson

IN A DRY SEASON

READER'S DIGEST SELECT EDITIONS
CONDENSED BOOKS DIVISION

Prologue

It was the Summer of Love, 1967, and I had just buried my husband when I first went back to see the reservoir that had flooded my childhood village.

I made the journey only a few months after Ronald and I had returned from one of our frequent long spells abroad. Spells that had suited me well for many years. Ronald, too, had suited me well. He was a decent man and a good husband, quite willing to accept that our marriage was one of convenience. I believe he saw me as an asset in his diplomatic career, though it was certainly neither my dazzling beauty nor my sparkling wit that had snared him. I was, however, presentable and intelligent, in addition to being an exceptionally good dancer.

Whatever the reason, I became adept at playing the minor diplomat's wife. It seemed a small price to pay. In a way, I was Ronald's passport to career success and promotion, and—though I never told him this—he was my passport to flight and escape. I had married him because I knew we would spend our lives far away from England, and I wanted to be as far away from England as possible. Now, after more than ten years abroad, it didn't matter very much. I would be quite happy to live out my days in the Belsize Park flat. Ronald, always a shrewd investor, had left me a tidy sum of money. Enough, at least, to live on for some years and to buy myself a new

Triumph sports car. A red one. With a radio.

Singing along with 'All You Need Is Love', I headed back to Hobb's End for the first time in over twenty years. For some reason I enjoyed the raw, naive and whimsical new music the young people were listening to, even though I was in my early forties. It made me long to be young again: young without the complications of my own youth; young without the war; young without the heartbreak.

I don't think I saw another car after I left the main road outside Skipton. It was one of those perfect summer days when the air smells sweet with the perfume of grass and flowers. I fancied I could even smell the warm exhalations of the dry-stone walls. Berries shone like polished garnets on the rowan trees and sheep bleated their plaintive calls from the far dalesides. The colours were all so vibrant—the green greener than ever, the blue of the sky piercingly bright.

Not far beyond Grassington I lost my way. I stopped and asked two men repairing a dry-stone wall. It was a long time since I had heard the characteristic broad speech of the Dales and at first it sounded foreign to me. Finally I understood, thanked them and left.

The old lane stopped at the edge of the woods, so I had to get out and walk the rest of the way along a crooked dirt path. Clouds of gnats whined above my head, wrens flitted through the undergrowth and bluetits hopped from branch to branch.

At last I broke out of the woods and stood at the edge of the reservoir. My heart started to pound, and for a moment I thought I was going to faint. But it passed.

When I had lived there, Hobb's End had been a village in a valley. Now I gazed upon a lake surrounded by forest.

The water's surface, utterly still, reflected the trees and the occasional shadow of a gull or a swallow flying over. To my right, I could see the small dam where the old river narrowed as it flowed into Harksmere. I sat on the bank and stared over the scene.

I was sitting where the old railway branch line used to be, a single track that ran to and from Harrogate, our only real access to the larger world beyond Hobb's End during the war. Many a time had I waited on the platform with rising excitement to hear the distant chugging and whistling of the old steam engine.

As I sat there remembering, time went by. I had started out late

from London. Soon, darkness infused the woods around me. A whisper of a breeze sprang up. Then a full moon rose, scattering its bone-white light, in which I fancied I could see clear through the water to the village that used to be there.

I saw a vision of the village as it had been when I lived there, smoke curling from chimneys over the slate and flagstone roofs, the dark mill at the west end, the squat church tower, the High Street curving beside the narrow river, people going about their daily business. In my vision, I could even see our little shop, where I met her for the first time that blustery spring day in 1941.

Chapter One

Adam Kelly loved to play in the derelict houses, loved the musty smell of the old rooms, the way they creaked and groaned as he moved. He loved to leap the gaps between the broken stairs, and hop from rafter to rafter, kicking up plaster dust.

This afternoon, Adam had a whole village to play in.

He stood at the rim of the shallow valley, staring at the ruins below. This was the day he had been waiting for. The future of the universe depended on Adam today; the village was a test, one of the things he had to conquer before advancing to the Seventh Level.

The only other people in sight stood at the far end, near the old flax mill: a man in jeans and a red T-shirt and a woman dressed all in white. They were pretending to be tourists, pointing their video camera here and there, but Adam suspected they might be after the same thing he was. He had played the game often enough on his computer to know that things were never what they seemed.

He half slid and half ran down the dirt slope, skidding to a halt when he reached the red, baked earth at the bottom. The sun beat down and made him sweat at the back of his neck. His glasses kept slipping down his nose. The Talisman was here somewhere, and it was Adam's job to find it. But where to begin? He didn't even know what it looked like, only that there must be clues somewhere.

He crossed the old stone bridge and walked into one of the half-demolished cottages. It smelt like a bad toilet.

Sunlight slanted in through the space where the roof had been. In places, the heavy stone flags that formed the floor had shifted and cracked, and thick gobbets of mud oozed up between them.

There was nothing in this house. Time to move on.

Outside, Adam noticed an outbuilding near the bridge, about seven feet high, with a slanting flagstone roof still intact, the kind of place that had perhaps once been used to store coal or keep food cold. Whatever it had been, The Destructors had left it largely alone. Here, at least, was a structure he could mount to get a clear view.

On one side a number of stones stuck out like steps. Carefully, Adam rested his weight on the first one. It was slippy, but it held fast. He started to climb, and soon he was at the top.

He pulled himself onto the roof. It was easy enough to walk on. But when he got to the middle the thick stone slabs gave way beneath him. With a scream, he plunged down into the darkness.

He landed on his back on a cushion of mud; his left wrist cracked against a fallen flagstone and his right arm, stretched out to break his fall, sank up to the elbow.

As he lay there, winded, looking up at the square of blue sky above him, he saw two of the remaining roof slabs tilt and fall towards him, each one about three feet square and six inches thick, enough to smash him to a pulp if it hit him. But he couldn't move.

They seemed to drift down in slow motion. He felt no panic, no fear, just acceptance. He knew there was nothing he could do to avoid whatever fate had in store for him. This must be the Seventh Level, he thought as he held his breath, waiting for the impact.

One slab fell to his left and embedded itself in the mud; the other fell to his right and cracked in two against one of the floor flags.

So he had been spared. He felt light-headed. There was nothing seriously damaged, he thought, as he started to move his limbs slowly. His left wrist hurt a lot, but it didn't feel broken. His right arm was still thrust deep in the mud. He tried to wiggle his fingers under the mud and they brushed against something hard.

It felt like a cluster of smooth, hard spindles, or a bundle of short rods. Curious, he pushed his arm in deeper and grasped the object tightly; then he tugged. The mud made sucking, slurping sounds as, inch by inch, he dragged his arm free. Finally, he was able to see the object he was holding.

It was the skeleton of a hand.

BANKS STEPPED BACK to survey his handiwork, whistling along with the habanera from *Carmen*, which was playing loudly on the stereo. Not bad for an amateur, he thought, dropping the paint-brush in a bowl of turpentine, and a definite improvement over the mildewed wallpaper he had stripped from the walls of his new home yesterday.

He particularly liked the colour. The man at the DIY centre said it was calming, and Banks needed all the calming he could get. The shade of blue reminded him of the Greek island of Santorini, which he and his estranged wife Sandra had visited. He hadn't bargained on that memory, but he thought he could live with it.

Pleased with himself, Banks pulled a packet of cigarettes from his top pocket. Only three gone since morning. Good. He was trying to restrict himself to ten a day or less. He walked into the kitchen and put the kettle on for a cup of tea. The telephone rang.

Banks turned off the stereo and picked up the receiver.

'Dad?'

'Brian, is that you? I've been trying to get in touch with you. Where are you?'

'I'm staying at Andrew's flat.'

'Where?'

'Wimbledon. Look, Dad . . .'

'Isn't it about time your exam results were out?'

'Yeah, well, that's why I was calling you . . .'

'Go on,' Banks prompted. 'You *did* pass, didn't you?'

'Course I did. It's just that I didn't do as well as I expected.'

'What did you get?'

Brian almost whispered. 'A third.'

'A *third*? That's a bit of a disappointment, isn't it?'

'Yeah, well, it's more than you ever got.'

Banks took a deep breath. 'It doesn't matter a damn what I did or didn't get. It's you we're talking about. Your future. You'll never get a job with a third-class degree. Do you want to be another statistic? Another unemployed yobbo?'

'Thanks a lot, Dad. Nice to know you believe in me. Anyway, as a matter of fact, I'm not on the dole. We're going to try and make a go of it. Me and the band.'

'You're *what*?'

'Andrew knows this bloke who's got a studio, like, and he's said we can go down and make a demo of some of my songs. People like us. We've got gigs coming out of our ears. We're making plenty of money.'

'Money's not everything. What about the future? What are you going to do when you've peaked at twenty-five and you don't have a penny in the bank? Have you talked to your mother about this?'

'Well, I sort of thought, maybe . . . you could do that.'

Him talk to Sandra? They couldn't even discuss the weather these days without an argument.

The kettle started whistling.

'I think you'd better ring her yourself,' he said.

'Thanks a lot, Dad,' Brian said, his voice hard-edged with bitterness. 'I thought you'd understand. I thought you *liked* music. Go see to your kettle.'

'Brian—'

But Brian hung up. Hard. Banks stormed into the kitchen and turned the kettle off. He didn't even feel like a cup of tea any more.

Before he had a chance to think any further, the phone rang again.

This time it was Chief Constable Jeremiah 'Jimmy' Riddle. Must be my lucky day, Banks thought. The new call also meant that Banks couldn't dial 1471 to get Brian's Wimbledon phone number, which he had neglected to ask for. He cursed and reached for his cigarettes again. At this rate he'd never stop. Bugger it. He lit up.

'Skiving off again, are you, Banks?'

'Holiday,' said Banks. 'It's official. You can check.'

'Doesn't matter. I've got a job for you to do. Now.'

Banks wondered what kind of job Jimmy Riddle would call him off his holidays for. Ever since Riddle had had to reinstate him reluctantly after dishing out a hasty suspension the previous year,

Banks had been in career Siberia, his life a treadmill of reports. Not one active investigation in nine months. Surely the situation wasn't going to change this easily? There had to be more to it; Riddle never made a move without a hidden agenda.

'We've just got a report in from Harkside,' Riddle went on. 'A young lad found some bones at the bottom of Thornfield Reservoir. It dried up over the summer. Used to be a village there, I gather. Anyway, there's nothing but a section station in Harkside, and all they've got is a lowly detective sergeant. I want you down there as senior investigating officer.'

'Old bones? Can't it wait?'

'Probably. But I'd rather you get started right away.'

'What about Harrogate or Ripon?'

'Too busy. Don't be so ungrateful, Banks. Here's the perfect opportunity for you to drag your career out of the slump it's fallen into. You'll find the local DS already at the scene. Cabbot's the name.'

Banks stopped to think. What the hell was going on here? A detective chief inspector would not, under normal circumstances, be dispatched to the remote borders of the county simply to examine a pile of old bones. Riddle was clearly not doing him any favours; he must have got tired of confining Banks to the station and had thought up some new and interesting way to torture him. He obviously believed the case would be boring and unpleasant, and that it would lead to certain failure and embarrassment.

'And, Banks. Don't forget your wellies.'

Banks could have sworn he heard Riddle snigger.

He dug out a map of the Yorkshire Dales. Thornfield was the westernmost in a chain of three linked reservoirs built along the River Rowan, which ran more or less east from its source high in the Pennines until it turned south and joined the River Wharfe near Otley. Banks traced a route on the map. Getting there would probably take an hour or more.

After a quick shower, Banks picked up his car keys and wallet, then walked out into the afternoon sunshine. Before setting off, he stood for a moment, resting his hands on the warm stone wall, and looked down at the bare rocks where the Gratly waterfalls should be. A quote from a T. S. Eliot poem came to his mind:

'Thoughts of a dry brain in a dry season.' Very apt. It had been a long drought; everything was dry that summer, including Banks's thoughts.

He wished his conversation with Brian hadn't ended the way it had. Well, he thought, getting into the Cavalier, Brian was old enough to make his own decisions. If he wanted to chuck everything in for a shot at fame and fortune, that was up to him, wasn't it?

At least Banks had a real job to do. Jimmy Riddle had made a mistake this time. No doubt he believed he had given Banks a filthy, dead-end job; but he had overlooked the one overriding characteristic Banks possessed, even at his lowest ebb: *curiosity*. Feeling, for a moment, like a grounded pilot suddenly given permission to fly again, Banks drove off.

THE BOOK SIGNING STARTED at half past six, but Vivian Elmsley had told her publicist, Wendi, that she liked to arrive early, get familiar with the place and have a chat with the staff.

There was already a crowd at a quarter past. All of a sudden, after twenty novels in as many years, Vivian Elmsley was a *success*. Her Detective Inspector Niven series had made it to the small screen; the first three episodes had been shown, to great critical acclaim, and Vivian had become about as familiar a face to the general public as a writer ever is. She had been interviewed by Melvyn Bragg on *The South Bank Show* and had featured prominently in *Woman's Own* magazine. After all, becoming an 'overnight success' in one's seventies was quite newsworthy.

At 6.30 on the dot, Adrian, the event organiser, introduced her, and to a smattering of applause Vivian picked up her copy of the latest Inspector Niven story and began to read. About five minutes was enough, she reckoned. Anything less made her look as if she couldn't wait to get away; anything more risked losing the audience's attention.

After the reading, people formed an orderly queue, and Vivian signed their books, pausing to chat briefly with everyone, asking if they wanted any specific sort of dedication and making sure she spelt their names right.

Vivian looked down at her hand as she signed. Talon-like, almost skeletal, dotted with liver spots. Hands were the first to go, she thought. The rest of her was remarkably well preserved. She had remained tall and lean. She hadn't shrunk or run to fat like so many elderly women. Steel-grey hair, pulled back tightly and fastened at the back, created a widow's peak over her strong, thin face; her deep blue eyes were almost oriental in their slant, her nose was slightly hooked and her lips thin. Not a face that smiled often, people thought. And they were right, even though it had not always been so.

'You used to live up north, didn't you?'

Vivian looked up, startled. The man appeared to be about sixty, thin to the point of emaciation, with a long, gaunt, pale face and lank fair hair. He was wearing faded jeans and a gaudy, short-sleeved shirt. He held the book out for her to sign.

Vivian nodded. 'A long time ago.' Then she looked at the book. 'Who would you like me to sign this to?'

'What was the name of the place where you lived?'

'It was a long time ago.'

'Did you go by the same name then?'

'Look, I—'

'Excuse me, sir.' It was Adrian, politely asking the man to move along. He did as he was asked, and left.

Adrian brought Vivian a glass of wine and she carried on signing.

When it was all over, Adrian and the staff suggested dinner, but Vivian was tired. All she wanted to do was go home to a long hot bath and a gin and tonic.

'I'll drive you home,' said Wendi.

Vivian laid her hand on Wendi's forearm. 'No, my dear,' she said. 'I'll be perfectly all right. I'm not over the hill yet.'

Wendi blushed. She had probably been told that Vivian was prickly. Someone always warned the publicists.

'I'm sorry. I didn't mean to suggest anything like that. It's my job.'

'A pretty young girl like you must have far better things to do than drive an old lady home.'

Wendi smiled and looked at her watch. 'Well, perhaps if I phone my boyfriend we could get some last-minute theatre tickets. But only if you're sure.'

'Quite sure, my dear. Good night.'

As she walked to the tube, Vivian thought again about the strange man in the bookshop. She didn't like to dwell on the past but he had pushed her into a reminiscent mood, as had the recent newspaper photographs of the dried-up Thornfield Reservoir.

The ruins of Hobb's End were exposed to the light of day for the first time in over forty years, and the memories of her life there had come crowding back. Vivian shuddered as she walked down the steps to the underground.

BANKS PAUSED FOR BREATH after his walk through the woods. From where he stood on the edge of Thornfield Reservoir, the entire elongated bowl of ruins lay open below him, about a quarter of a mile wide and half a mile long. On the opposite embankment, the difference in soil colours showed where the water line had been. Beyond the high bank, Rowan Woods straggled away to the north.

The most dramatic part of the scene lay directly below: the sunken village itself, bracketed by a ruined mill on a hillock to the west, and by a tiny packhorse bridge to the east. There was no road surface, but the course of the old High Street by the river was easy enough to make out. It eventually forked at the bridge, one branch turning towards Rowan Woods, and the other continuing over the bridge, then out of the village along the embankment to Harkside.

Below him, a group of people stood by the other side of the bridge, one in uniform. It was a warm evening, and he was sweating by the time he got to the bottom of the narrow path. The valley bottom wasn't as muddy as it looked. Most of the exposed reddish-brown earth had been caked and cracked by the heat.

As he crossed the packhorse bridge, a woman walked towards him. 'Excuse me, sir,' she said. 'This is a crime scene. I'm afraid you can't come any further.'

Banks smiled. He knew he didn't look like a DCI. He wore a blue denim shirt open at the neck, with no tie, light tan trousers and black Wellington boots. 'Why isn't it taped off, then?' he asked.

The woman frowned. She was in her late twenties or early thirties, long-legged, tall and slim. She was wearing blue jeans and a herringbone jacket that followed the contours of her waist. Her chestnut hair fell in waves to her shoulders and she had a smooth, tanned complexion. She wasn't conventionally good-looking, but her looks showed character and intelligence. And the red wellies set it all off nicely.

Banks smiled. 'Do I have to throw you off the bridge before I can cross, like Robin Hood did to Little John?'

'I think you'll find it was the other way round, but you could try it,' she said. Then, after they had scrutinised one another for a few seconds, she squinted, and said, 'You'll be DCI Banks, then?'

'DS Cabbot, I presume?'

'Yes, sir.' She smiled. It was no more than a twitch of her mouth and a brief flash of light behind her eyes, but it left an impression.

'And these people?' Banks pointed to the man and woman talking to the uniformed policeman. The man was aiming a video camera at the outbuilding.

'They were scouting the location for a TV programme when they saw the boy fall. They ran to help him. Seems they also had their camera handy. I suppose it'll make a nice little item on the evening news.' She scratched the side of her nose. 'We'd run out of crime-scene tape at the section station, sir.'

'There's nothing we can do about the TV people now,' Banks said. 'You'd better explain to me what happened. All I know is that a boy discovered some old bones here.'

DS Cabbot nodded. 'Adam Kelly. He's thirteen. I sent him home. He seemed a bit shaken up, and he'd bruised his wrist and elbow. Nothing serious. He was walking on the roof and it gave way under him. Lucky he didn't break his back.' She pointed at the outbuilding. 'The rafters must have rotted. Anyway, the mud broke his fall, his arm got stuck in it, and he pulled up a skeleton of a hand.'

'Human?'

'Don't know, sir. I mean, it *looks* human to me, but we'll need an expert to be certain. I've read that it's easy to mistake bear paws for human hands.'

'*Bear paws?* When was the last time you saw a bear around these parts?'

'Why, just last week, sir.'

Banks paused a moment, saw the glint in her eye and smiled.

There was something about this woman that intrigued him. Most junior police officers, when questioned about their actions by a senior, generally either let a little of the 'Did I do the right thing, sir?' creep into their tone, or they became defensive. But DS Cabbot simply stated things as they had occurred, completely self-assured without being at all arrogant or insubordinate.

'Right,' he said, 'let's go and have a look.'

DS Cabbot led the way. Banks followed her to the outbuilding.

It was about six or seven feet square. Banks stood in the doorway and looked at the depression in the mud where the boy had landed, then at the two heavy slabs of stone on either side. DS Cabbot was right; Adam Kelly had been very lucky indeed.

His gaze alighted on the skeletal hand curled round the edge of a broken stone slab. The bones were dark and clotted with mud, but it looked like a human hand.

'We'd better get some experts in,' he said. 'Then we'll need a forensic anthropologist. In the meantime, I haven't had my tea yet. Is there somewhere nearby we might be able to get a bite?'

'The Black Swan in Harkside's your best bet.'

'Have you eaten?'

'No, but—'

'You can come with me, then, fill me in over a meal.'

VIVIAN ELMSLEY FELT bone-weary when she got home from the signing. She put her briefcase down in the hall and walked through to the living room. Most people would have been surprised at the modern chrome-and-glass decor, but she far preferred it to the antiques and knick-knacks that so often cluttered up old people's houses.

She poured a stiff gin and tonic and made her way to her favourite armchair. Supported by chrome tubes, upholstered in black leather, it leaned back at just the right angle to make reading, drinking or watching television sinfully comfortable.

Vivian glanced at the clock. Almost nine. She would watch the news first. After that, she would have her bath and read.

The news was the usual rubbish. Politics, for the most part, a botched assassination attempt in the Middle East. Then, towards the end, came one of those little human-interest bites.

This one made Vivian sit up and take notice.

The camera panned a cluster of familiar ruins as the voice-over explained that the drought had brought the lost Dales village of Hobb's End to light for the first time since it had been flooded in 1953. The camera angle changed, and she could see a group of people standing by the bridge.

'Today,' the voice-over went on, 'a young boy exploring the scene discovered something he hadn't bargained for.'

It was a mystery worthy of Miss Marple, the narrator went on, part of a skeleton was discovered, not in a cupboard, folks, but under the muddy floor of an old outbuilding. How could it have got there? The police were refusing to comment at this early stage.

Vivian let her body sag in the chair, and took a deep breath. Then she reached for her gin and tonic. The programme was well into the weather forecast by the time she had recovered from the shock.

When she felt a little calmer, she went into the study and dug through her filing cabinet for the manuscript she had written in the early 1970s, a few years after her last visit to Thornfield Reservoir. She carried it back through to the living room. It had never been intended for publication. In many ways, it had been a practice piece, one she had written when she became interested in writing after her husband's death. She had written it when she thought the old adage 'Write about what you know' meant 'Write about your own life'. Now she still wrote about what she knew—guilt, grief, pain, madness—only she put it into the lives of her characters.

As she started to read, she realised she wasn't sure exactly what it was. A memoir? A novella? She had tried to stick to the facts, had even consulted her old diaries for accuracy. But because she had written it at a time in her life when she had been unclear about the blurred line between autobiography and fiction, she couldn't be sure which was which. Would she see it any more clearly now? There was only one way to find out.

DS CABBOT LED the way to Harkside in her metallic purple Astra, and Banks followed her along the winding streets lined with limestone and gritstone cottages.

They parked beside the village green, where a few scattered trees provided shade for the benches. Old people sat in the late-summer dusk as the shadows grew long, watching the world go by. The essentials were arrayed around the green: a bank, newsagent's, butcher's, grocer's, a fifteenth-century church and three pubs.

'Do you live here?' Banks asked.

'For my sins, yes, sir.'

They walked over to the Black Swan, a whitewash-and-timber façade with gables and a sagging slate roof. Inside, a few tourists and ramblers lingered over after-dinner drinks at rickety wooden tables. Banks walked to the bar with DS Cabbot, who asked the barmaid if they could still get food.

'Depends what you want, love,' she said, and pointed to a list on the blackboard.

Banks decided on a beef and Stilton pie with chips. DS Cabbot ordered a salad sandwich, no chips.

'Diet?' Banks asked.

'No, sir. I don't eat meat. And the chips are cooked in animal fat. There's not a lot of choice.'

'I see. Drink?'

'Like a fish.' She laughed. 'Actually, I'll have a pint of Swan's Down Bitter. I'd recommend it very highly.'

Banks took her advice and was glad that he did. He had never met a vegetarian beer aficionado before.

They took their pints over to a table by the open window and Banks fished out his cigarettes. 'Do you mind?' he asked.

She shook her head. 'I usually manage to control my cravings.'

'Reformed?'

'A year.'

Banks lit up. 'I'm thinking of stopping soon myself.'

'Best of luck.' DS Cabbot took a sip of beer and smacked her lips. 'Ah, that's good. Do you mind if I ask you something?'

'No.'

She leaned forward and touched the hair at his right temple. 'What's that? The blue bit. I didn't think DCIs went in for dye jobs.'

Banks felt himself blush. He touched the spot she had indicated. 'It must be paint. I thought I'd washed it all off.'

She smiled. 'Never mind. Looks quite nice, actually.'

Banks tried to concentrate on the job at hand. 'I called my sergeant on the way here,' he said. 'He'll organise a team to dig out the bones tomorrow morning. A bloke called John Webb will be in charge. He's studied archaeology so he ought to know what he's doing. You can phone around the universities in the morning, see if you can come up with a friendly forensic anthropologist. In the meantime, tell me all about Thornfield Reservoir.'

DS Cabbot leaned back in her chair and crossed her legs. She had swapped her red wellies for a pair of white sandals, and her jeans rode up to reveal tapered ankles, bare except for a thin gold chain round the left one. Banks wondered again what she could possibly have done to end up in such a godforsaken outpost as Harkside.

'Thornfield Reservoir was created in the early fifties,' she began. 'The village had already been empty a few years by then. Since the end of the war, I think. It was called Hobb's End.'

Their meals arrived. Banks stubbed out his cigarette. 'Why was it empty? What drove people away?'

'Nothing drove them away. It just died. Places do. The flax mill was the village's *raison d'être* in the nineteenth century. The mill owner, Lord Clifford, also owned the land and the cottages. Very feudal.'

'You seem to be an expert.'

'I read up on the area when I came here. Anyway, the flax mill started to lose business—too much competition—and old Lord Clifford died. After the Second World War people moved away to the cities or to the other dales. Finally, the new Lord Clifford sold the land to Leeds Corporation Waterworks. They rehoused the remaining tenants, and over the next few years they created the reservoir.'

'So our body, if indeed there is one, and if it's human, has to have been down there since before the early fifties?'

'Unless someone put it there this summer.'

'I'm no expert, but from what I've seen it looks older than that.'

'Whoever buried it there could have moved it from somewhere else.'

'I suppose it's possible.'

'Whatever happened, there's no way a body could have got under those stone slabs on the outbuilding floor without a little human intervention, don't you think, sir?'

IT WAS A BLUSTERY AFTERNOON in April 1941, when she appeared in our shop for the first time. Even in her land girl uniform of green V-neck pullover, biscuit-coloured blouse, green tie and brown corduroy knee breeches, she looked like a film star.

She wasn't very tall, perhaps about five foot two or three, and the drab uniform couldn't hide the kind of figure I've heard men whistle at in the street. She had a pale, heart-shaped face, perfectly proportioned nose and mouth, and the biggest, deepest, bluest eyes I had ever seen. Her blonde hair cascaded from her brown felt hat. I was immediately put in mind of Hardy's novel, *A Pair of Blue Eyes*. Like Elfride Swancourt's, this land girl's eyes were 'a misty and shady blue, that had no beginning or surface . . . looked *into* rather than *at*'.

'I don't suppose you've got five Woodbines, have you?' she asked.

I shook my head. 'Sorry, we don't have any cigarettes at all.' It was one of the toughest times we'd had in the war thus far: the Luftwaffe was bombing our cities to ruins, the U-boats were sinking Atlantic convoys and the meat ration had been dropped to one and tenpence a week, but here she was, bold as brass, a stranger asking for cigarettes! I was lying, of course. We did have cigarettes, but what small supply we had we kept for our regular customers.

She broke into a bright smile. 'I didn't think you would have,' she said, 'but it was worth asking. Oh well, can't be helped.'

'Are you the new land girl at Top Hill Farm?' I asked, curious now.

She smiled again. 'Word gets around quickly, doesn't it? That's me. Gloria Stringer.' Then she held her hand out. Her hand was soft and slightly moist, like a summer leaf after rain. Mine felt coarse and heavy wrapped around such a delicate thing. 'Gwen Shackleton,' I muttered. 'Pleased to meet you.'

Gloria looked around. 'Not a lot to do here, is there?'

I smiled. 'Not a lot.' I knew what she meant, but it still struck me as an odd thing to say. I got up at six o'clock every morning to run the shop, and on top of that spent one night a week fire-watching. I also helped with the local Women's Voluntary Service.

I had heard how hard a land girl's job was, of course, but to judge by her appearance, you would swear that Gloria Stringer had never done a day's hard physical labour in her life. But in this, as in most of my first impressions about Gloria, I was quite wrong. She could spend the day haymaking, threshing, milking, snagging turnips, yet always appear fresh and alive, with energy to spare.

On first impressions, she struck me as being vain, common, shallow and selfish. Not to mention beautiful, of course.

Then Michael Stanhope walked in.

Michael Stanhope was something of a village character. A fairly successful artist, somewhere, I'd guess, in his early fifties, he was wearing a rumpled white linen suit, a shabby lavender shirt and a crooked yellow bow tie. He also wore his ubiquitous broad-brimmed hat and carried a cane with a snake-head handle. As usual, he looked quite dissipated. He had at least three days' stubble on his face, and emanated a sort of general fug of stale smoke and alcohol.

A lot of people didn't like Michael Stanhope because he wasn't afraid to say what he thought and he spoke out against the war. I quite liked him, in a way, though I didn't agree with his views. Half the time he only said what he did to annoy people.

'Good morning, my cherub,' he said, as always, though I felt far from cherubic. 'I trust you have my usual?'

'Er, sorry, Mr Stanhope,' I stammered. 'We're all out.'

'All out? Come, come now, girl, that can't be. I'll bet if you looked in the usual place,' he said, leaning forward and rapping on the counter with his cane, 'you would find them.'

I knew when I was beaten. Mortified, I reached under the counter and brought out two packets of Piccadilly.

'That'll be one and eight, please,' I said.

'Outrageous,' Mr Stanhope complained as he dug out the coins, 'the way this government is taxing us to death to make war.'

When I glanced at Gloria guiltily, she smiled at me and shrugged. Mr Stanhope must have caught the gesture.

'Ah, I *see*,' he said, turning his gaze fully towards Gloria and admiring her figure quite openly. 'Do I take it that you were enquiring after cigarettes yourself, my dear?'

Gloria nodded. 'As a matter of fact, I was.'

'Well,' said Mr Stanhope, 'I'll tell you what, perhaps we can come to some sort of arrangement. I have but one stipulation.'

'Oh,' said Gloria, narrowing her eyes. 'And what might that be?'

'That you smoke in the street every now and then.'

Gloria started to laugh. 'That won't be a problem, I assure you.'

And he handed her one of the packets.

I was flabbergasted. Cigarettes weren't cheap or easy to get.

Instead of protesting that she couldn't possibly accept them, as I would have done, Gloria simply said, 'Why, thank you very much, Mr . . .?'

He beamed at her. 'Stanhope. Michael Stanhope. It's my pleasure, my dear. It's a rare treat indeed to meet a woman as comely as thyself around these parts.' Then he moved a step closer and scrutinised her, quite rudely, I thought, rather like a farmer looking over a horse he was about to buy.

Gloria stood her ground.

'You know, you really must visit my studio, my dear. See my etchings, as it were.' And with that, Mr Stanhope was gone.

In the silence that followed, Gloria and I stared at one another for a moment, then we both burst out giggling. I told her I was sorry for deceiving her, but she waved the apology aside. 'You have your regulars to attend to,' she said.

'I must apologise for Mr Stanhope, too,' I said. 'I'm afraid he can be quite rude.'

'Nonsense,' she said. 'I rather liked him. And he did give me these.'

She opened the packet and offered me a cigarette. I shook my head. She put one in her mouth and lit it with a small silver lighter. 'I can see these will have to last me a while.'

'I can put some aside for you in future,' I said.

'Would you? Oh, yes, please! That would be wonderful. Now if I might just have a look at that copy of *Picture Goer* over there, the one with Vivien Leigh on the cover—'

But before I could get the magazine for her, Matthew dashed in.

Gloria turned at the sound of the bell, eyebrows raised in curiosity. When he saw her, my brother stopped in his tracks and fell into her eyes so deeply you could hear the splash.

THE FIRST THING Banks did when he got back to the cottage that night was check the answering machine. Nothing. Damn it. He wanted to put things right after his miserable cockup on the phone earlier that day, but he still had no access to Brian's number in Wimbledon. Sandra might know, of course, but the last thing he wanted to do was talk to her.

Banks poured himself a whisky, lit the last cigarette of the day and took his drink outside. The cottage stood on a narrow, unpaved lane about fifty yards west of Gratly. Before the drought it had been an ideal spot for ramblers to stop and admire the falls, but at night there was never anyone there. Banks liked to stand out there in the evening. It helped him to think, get things sorted.

Tonight, sharp starlight pricked the satin sky, along with the lights of a distant farmhouse; a gibbous moon hung over the valley, and the square church tower stood solid against the night.

Banks thought again about the odd way he'd come to live in this isolated limestone cottage. Over his last few months alone in the Eastvale semi, he had drifted so far from himself that he hadn't even cleaned or tidied the place. He spent most of his evenings out in pubs and his nights falling asleep half-drunk on the sofa, take-away cartons piling up in an ever-widening circle around him. In April he seemed to reach his lowest ebb. There was a new man in Sandra's life, a photojournalist called Sean. As a result, Banks was full of anger and self-pity. When Sandra decided that their separation was to be permanent, they sold the semi.

After the sale, Banks began to seek isolation. When he first saw the cottage from the outside, he didn't think much of it. The view of the dale was terrific, but it was a squat, ugly little place that needed a lot of work. A typical Dales mix of limestone, grit and flag, it had originally been a farm labourer's cottage. Inside, the place smelt of camphor and mould, and all the furniture and decor seemed dark and dingy. Downstairs was a living room with a stone fireplace at one end; upstairs, only two small bedrooms. But when he walked into the kitchen he experienced a feeling of well-being and peace. He *knew* he had to have the cottage.

The cottage became his long-term project—his therapy, and his refuge. Working on the cottage was like working on himself. Both needed renovating, and both had a long way to go. Somehow he had lost his way over the past year, and he wanted to find a new one. So far, he had fitted some pine cupboards in the kitchen, installed a shower unit, and painted the living room. It hadn't kept the depression away completely, but made it more manageable.

Banks stubbed out his cigarette and went back inside. As he got ready for bed, he thought of the skeletal hand, possibly human; of DS Cabbot, definitely human; and of Hobb's End, that lost, ruined village suddenly risen from the depths with its secrets.

Chapter Two

Banks watched from the edge of the woods the next morning as the Scene of Crime Officers slowly lifted the skeleton from its muddy grave under the expert direction of John Webb.

First, they had to take down the wall next to which the bones were buried, then they made a trench around the area and dug down until the bones were exposed, about three feet below the surface. Next they slipped a thin sheet of metal into the earth under the bones, and finally they got it in place, ready to lift out.

The bones came up on the metal sheet, still packed in earth, and four SOCO pallbearers carried it up the slope, where they laid it out on the grass at Banks's feet. It was just eleven and DS Cabbot still hadn't shown up. Banks had already talked to Adam Kelly, who hadn't been able to add anything to his previous statement. He was still shaken, but Banks sensed a resilience in him. The little adventure had done him no lasting harm, and he would enjoy celebrity status among his school pals for a while.

Banks stared at the filthy, twisted shape at his feet. The bones had taken on the muddy brown colour of the earth they had lain in for so long. The skull looked full of it—mud in the mouth, the nose, the eye sockets—and some of the long bones looked like rusted metal pipes.

The SOCOs had already photographed the skeleton during every stage of its excavation and now went back down and started their detailed search of the area, digging deeper and further afield. John Webb also searched through the dirt for any objects that had been buried at the same time.

Banks leaned against a tree trunk and watched Webb work. He

was tired; most of the night he had tossed and turned, and the morning heat made him drowsy. Giving in to the feeling for a moment, he closed his eyes and rested his head on the tree. He was at the edge of sleep when he heard a rustling behind him, then a voice.

'Morning, sir. Rough night?'

'Something like that,' said Banks, moving away from the tree.

'Sorry I've been so long,' said DS Cabbot. 'A lot of university profs are still away on holiday. Anyway, I've tracked down a Dr Ioan Williams, University of Leeds, a physical anthropologist with experience in forensic work. He said if we could get the remains to the university lab, he'd manage a preliminary look by early evening.'

'Good,' said Banks. 'The sooner we know what we're dealing with here, the better.'

If the skeleton had been lying there for a hundred years or more, the investigation wouldn't really be worth pursuing. On the other hand, *if* it turned out to be a murder victim, buried there during or since the war, there was a chance that the killer was still alive.

'Want me to supervise the move?' Webb asked.

Banks nodded. 'If you would, John.'

Webb looked at his watch. 'With any luck, we can have it in the lab by one o'clock.'

'I need to know a lot more about the village,' Banks said to DS Cabbot. He pointed towards the ruins of the cottage near the bridge. 'The outbuilding clearly belonged to that cottage, so I'd like to know who lived there and who the neighbours were. It seems to me that we've got three possibilities. Someone used the empty village as a dumping spot to bury a body during the time it was in disuse—'

'Between May 1946 and August 1953. I checked.'

'Right. Or the body was buried while the village was still occupied, before May 1946, and the victim was buried not far from home. Or it was put there this summer. It's too soon for speculation, but we do need to know who lived in that cottage before the village emptied out, and if anyone from the village was reported missing.'

'Yes, sir.'

'Where are the parish records now?'

'I don't know. I imagine they were moved to St Jude's in Harkside.'

'They might be worth a look if you draw a blank elsewhere. There's the local newspaper, too. And, DS Cabbot?'

'Sir?'

'Look, I can't keep calling you DS Cabbot. What's your first name?'

She smiled. 'Annie, sir. Annie Cabbot.'

'Right, Annie Cabbot, do you happen to know how many doctors or dentists there were in Hobb's End?'

'I shouldn't imagine there were many. Most people probably went to Harkside.'

'Try to find out, anyway. It's a long shot, but if we can find any dental records matching the remains, we'll be in luck.'

'I'll look into it, sir. And what should I do next year?'

Banks smiled. 'I'm sure you can conscript one of your PCs to help. Do you happen to know if anyone who lived in Hobb's End is still alive, maybe living in Harkside now?'

'I'll ask Inspector Harmond. He grew up around these parts.'

'Good. I'll leave you to it and see these bones off to Leeds with John. Meet me at the lab at six o'clock. In the meantime,' he said, 'here's my mobile number. Ring me if you come up with anything.'

'Right you are, sir.'

BANKS WAS AN ODD FISH, Annie thought as she drove back to Harkside. She'd heard a few rumours. She knew, for example, that Chief Constable Riddle hated him, that Banks was under a cloud, though she didn't know why. Someone had even hinted at fisticuffs between the two. Whatever the reason, his career was on hold.

Annie had also heard that Banks's wife had left him not too long ago. Not only that, but there were stories going around that he had a woman in Leeds. She had heard him described as a loner and a skiver. He was a brilliant detective gone to seed, they said, over the hill and burnt out since his wife left.

On first impressions, Annie liked him. She certainly found him attractive, and he didn't look much older than mid-thirties, despite the scattering of grey at the temples of his closely cropped black hair. He seemed tired, but she could sense that the fire still smouldered somewhere behind his sharp blue eyes. On the other hand, perhaps the fire she sensed was simply embers, just about to cave in on themselves. Well, if Annie had learned one thing over the past couple of years, it was not to jump to conclusions about anyone.

She parked beside the section station and walked inside. Only four of them worked directly out of the station: Inspector Harmond, Annie and PCs Cameron and Gould. They seemed a pretty decent bunch of men, as men go. She certainly felt no threat from any of them. PC Cameron was married with two kids, to whom he was clearly devoted. Gould seemed to be one of those rare types who have no sexual dimension whatsoever, content to live at home with his mum and add stamps to his album. Inspector Harmond was, well, avuncular.

The office area of Harkside police station was open-plan—apart from Inspector Harmond's office, partitioned off at the far end. Annie's desk took up a corner, part of which included a side window. It wasn't much of a view, only the cobbled alley, a gate and the back wall of the Three Feathers, but at least she was close to a source of light and air. These little things mattered so much, Annie had discovered. She had had her shot at the big time, the fast track, with all its excitement, but it had ended badly for her. Now she was slowly rediscovering what mattered in life.

Harkside was generally a law-abiding sort of community, so there wasn't a lot for a detective sergeant to do. There was plenty of paperwork to keep her occupied, but it was hardly a high-overtime posting, and there were slack periods. That also suited her fine.

She headed first to the coffee machine and filled her mug, then she knocked on Inspector Harmond's door.

Harmond looked up from his desk. 'Annie. What is it, lass?'

'Got a minute?'

'Aye. Sit down.'

In his early fifties, Harmond seemed content to be a rural inspector for the rest of his working life. He had a pleasant, open face. The features were a bit coarse, and a few black hairs grew out of the end of his misshapen potato nose, but it was the kind of face you could trust.

'It's this skeleton thing,' she said, sitting. 'DCI Banks wanted to know if anyone who used to live in Hobb's End lives here now.'

Harmond scratched his temple. 'You remember Mrs Kettering, the one whose budgie escaped?'

'How could I forget?' It had been one of Annie's first cases in Harkside.

Inspector Harmond smiled. 'I know she used to live in Hobb's End. Remember where she is now?'

'Up on the Edge, isn't it?'

The Edge was what the locals called the fifty-foot embankment that ran along the south side of Harksmere Reservoir. Only one row of cottages overlooked the water, separated from the rest of Harkside village by about half a mile of open countryside.

'Anyone else?'

'Not that I can think of. Not offhand, at any rate. Leave it with me, I'll ask around. You'll keep me informed?'

'I will.'

'And, Annie?' Harmond scratched the side of his nose. 'This DCI Banks. I've heard a bit about him. Better watch yourself, lass.'

BEFORE I TELL YOU what happened next, let me tell you a little about myself and my village. My name, as you already know, is Gwen Shackleton, which is short for Gwynneth. My father died before the war began, and by 1940 my mother was an invalid, suffering from rheumatoid arthritis. Sometimes she was able to help out in the shop, but the brunt of the work fell to me.

Matthew helped me as much as he could, but university kept him busy most of the week and the Home Guard took up his weekends. He was twenty-one, but despite the call-up the Ministry was encouraging him to finish his engineering degree at Leeds University. They believed that his training would come in useful in the forces.

Our little newsagent's-cum-general store was about halfway along the High Street, and we lived above it. We didn't sell perishable goods, just things like newspapers, sweets, cigarettes, tea and tinned goods—depending, of course, on what was available.

Though most of the able-bodied men had joined up, the village had never seemed busier. The old flax mill was operating at full strength and most of the married women worked there. The military wanted flax for parachute harnesses and other things.

There was also a big RAF base about a mile away, and the High Street was often busy with Jeeps and lorries. The airmen sometimes came to the village pub—the Shoulder of Mutton—except when they went to Harkside, where there was much more to do.

These things aside, though, I think that at first the war impinged upon us very little. Even with rationing, our diets didn't change as much as those of city folks, for we had been used to eating plenty of vegetables, and in the country there were always eggs, butter and milk.

Perhaps the hardest thing to get used to was the blackout. We had to tape up our windows to prevent damage from broken glass, and we also had to hang up the heavy blackout curtains. On moonlit nights, especially if there was a full moon, the effect could be spectacular: the hills were dusted with silver powder, and the stars glittered like cut diamonds on black velvet. But on cloudy or moonless nights, people bumped into trees and even cycled into the river. You could use a torch if you wrapped the light with several layers of tissue paper, but batteries were scarce. All car and bicycle lights had to be masked, too. There were a lot of car accidents, until petrol became too scarce and nobody drove any more except on business.

The day before Gloria Stringer arrived, the war hit closer to home: Matthew got his call-up papers, and was due to report for his medical in Leeds in two weeks.

DS CABBOT WAS JUST PARKING her Astra when Banks arrived at Dr Williams's lab just off the main campus. He watched her get out and stepped up beside her.'

She turned. 'Ah, sir.'

Banks smiled and nodded towards the building. 'Let's go inside.'

He followed her up the steps. This evening she was wearing a mid-length black skirt and matching jacket over a white blouse. She was also carrying a black leather briefcase. Much more businesslike. Banks caught a brief whiff of jasmine as he walked behind her.

He pressed the intercom and got them buzzed in.

Dr Ioan Williams waited for them on the first-floor landing. He was a tall, rangy fellow with long, greasy blond hair and wire-rimmed glasses that magnified his grey eyes. Much younger than

Banks had expected, Dr Williams wasn't wearing a white lab coat but was dressed casually in jeans and a T-shirt advertising Guinness. His handshake was firm, and judging by the way he lingered over DS Cabbot, his mind was not 100 per cent focused on science.

'Come in,' he said, leading the way down the corridor and opening the lab door.

In the centre of the room the skeleton lay on a long table. The bones looked different now that Williams's assistants had been to work on them. Much of the crusting remained, but the skull, ribs and long bones were easier to examine. They were still a dirty yellow-brown, but at least the whole resembled something more like a human being.

'There are a number of odds and ends my lads found,' Williams said. 'They're over there on the bench.'

Banks looked at the collection of filthy objects on the lab bench along one wall. It was hard to make out what they were: A ring? Shreds of old clothing?

'Can you get them cleaned up and sent over?' he asked.

'No problem. Now let's get down to work.'

Annie took out her notebook.

'First of all,' Williams began, 'let me confirm, just for the record, that we *are* dealing with human remains, most likely Caucasian.'

'What about DNA analysis?' Banks asked.

Williams grunted. 'People seem to think DNA analysis is some sort of miracle answer. It's not. Right now, I can tell you a hell of a lot more than any DNA could. May I continue?'

'Please do. But get a DNA analysis done, anyway. It might be useful for determining identity.'

Williams nodded. 'Very well.' He turned back to the skeleton. 'The height of the subject was easy enough to determine: a hundred and fifty-five centimetres.'

'What's that in feet and inches?' Banks asked.

'Five foot two.' Dr Williams looked over and smiled at DS Cabbot. 'But I can't be sure about the eyes of blue.'

Annie gave him a chilly smile. Banks noticed her roll her eyes when Williams had turned away.

'Also, you are dealing with the remains of a young woman. In general,' Williams explained, 'a male skeleton is larger, the bone surfaces rougher. The male skull is thicker.'

'Well, what do you know,' Annie muttered.

Williams laughed. 'Anyway, in this case, the pelvis is intact, and that's the easiest way for the trained eye to tell. The female pelvis is wider and lower than the male's, to facilitate childbearing.' Williams ran his hand over the skeleton's pelvic bone. 'This pubic curve is definitely female, and here, the sciatic notch is also unmistakably female. Much wider than a male's.' He looked at DS Cabbot again, but Annie kept her head down.

Williams picked up a small magnifying glass from the lab bench and handed it to Banks. 'And look at this.' Williams pointed to where the two pelvic bones joined at the front of the body. Holding the glass Banks could just about make out a small groove.

'That's a parturition scar,' Williams said. 'It's caused by the stresses that attached ligaments put on the bone.'

'So she'd given birth to at least one child?'

'Well,' Williams went on, 'there's only a single pit on either side of the pubis, which would strongly suggest that she only gave birth once in her life.'

'How old was she when she died?'

'I'd have to do more comprehensive tests to be certain of that.'

'What do you have to go on at the moment?'

'Well, there's epiphysial union, for a start. Here, at the very ends of the long bones in both the arms and the legs, the epiphyses have all firmly united with the shafts, which doesn't usually happen until the age of twenty or twenty-one. But look here.' He pointed towards the collarbone. 'The epiphysis at the sternal end of the clavicle, which doesn't unite until the late twenties, has *not* united yet. So I'd say about twenty-two to twenty-eight.'

'Any idea how long she's been down there?'

Williams folded his arms. 'Well, there are certain indications that we're dealing with recent, as opposed to archaeological remains. What do you notice most about the bones?'

'The colour,' said Banks.

'Right. And what does that tell you?'

Banks wasn't too sure about the usefulness of the Socratic method at a time like this, but he had found that it is usually a good idea to humour scientists. 'That they're stained or decayed.'

'Good. Good. Actually, the discoloration is an indication that they have taken on some of the colour of the surrounding earth. Then there's this.' He pointed to several places on the skeleton. 'The bone surface is crumbling, or flaking. Now if you take all this into account, then I'd estimate it's been down there for a few decades. As we already know, it's unlikely she was buried after 1953. I'd go back about ten years from there.'

'Nineteen forty-three?'

'Hold on. This is a very rough guess. The rate of skeletal decay is wildly unpredictable. Obviously, an odontologist will be able to tell you a bit more, narrow things down, perhaps. There are a number of tests I can carry out. But I'll need more information about soil, mineral content, bacterial content, temperature fluctuations and various other factors. I'll visit the site first thing in the morning and take some samples.' He looked at Annie. 'Perhaps DS Cabbot here would be willing to escort me there?'

'Sorry,' said Annie. 'Far too busy.'

His eyes lingered on her. 'Pity.'

'Visiting the site's no problem,' Banks said. 'I'll arrange for a car and make sure the SOCOs are expecting you. Can you tell us anything at all about cause of death?'

'I think I can help you a little with that, though it's not really my area of expertise, and you should definitely get your Home Office pathologist to confirm this.'

'Of course.'

'See those markings on the bones there?' Dr Williams pointed to triangular notches on several of the ribs and the pelvic area.

Once Banks saw them he knew he'd seen them before. 'Stab wounds,' he muttered.

'Exactly. See those little curls of bone there, like wood shavings? They're still attached to the bone, and that only happens with living bone. There's no sign of healing. If she'd remained alive after these injuries, the bones would have healed to some extent, starting about ten days after the injury. Add to that the fact that the position of these wounds indicates the blade would certainly have pierced vital organs, and I'd conclude that she was stabbed viciously, more than once, almost certainly causing death.'

Banks looked at Annie Cabbot.

'Murder, then,' she said.

THE FOLLOWING MORNING Mrs Ruby Kettering was squatting in the garden spraying her dahlias. She looked up as Annie opened the gate and introduced herself.

'I know who you are,' the old lady said, placing her hands on her thighs and pushing herself to her feet. 'I remember you. You're that nice policewoman who found Joey, my budgie.'

Mrs Kettering was wearing a red baseball cap, a loose yellow smock and baggy white shorts down to her knees.

'What can I do for you?' she said, wiping the streaks of sweat and soil from her brow with her forearm.

'It's about Hobb's End. I understand you used to live there.'

Mrs Kettering nodded. 'Seven years Reg and me lived there. From 1933 to 1940. It was our first home together, just after we got married. Listen, dear, would you like a cold drink? Lemonade, perhaps?'

'Thank you.'

'We can sit over there,' Mrs Kettering said. She pointed to a flagstone patio where two deck chairs sat, half in the sun.

'That'll be just fine,' Annie said, walking over.

Mrs Kettering disappeared inside the house. Annie settled herself into one of the deck chairs, stretched out her legs and luxuriated.

'Here we are, dear,' said Mrs Kettering, coming back out with a tray. She offered a tall glass to Annie, then took the other for herself, set the tray aside and sat down.

'Hobb's End,' Mrs Kettering said. 'That takes me back. What do you want to know?'

'As much as you can tell me,' Annie said. And then she told Mrs Kettering about the skeleton.

'Yes, I saw something about that on the news. A young woman, about five foot two, with a baby?' Mrs Kettering repeated, brow knotted in concentration. 'Well, there was the McSorley lass, but she'd have been well over thirty by the time we left. No, dear, I can't honestly say anyone comes to mind. The far cottage, you say, the one by the fairy bridge?'

'Fairy bridge?'

'That's what we used to call it. Because it was so small, only fairies could cross over it.'

'I see. That's right.'

Mrs Kettering pulled a face. 'Sorry, love, it's a blank. I certainly don't remember any young woman living there.'

'Never mind,' said Annie. 'What can you tell me about the village itself? What sort of people lived there?'

'All sorts, really. Shopkeepers, milkmen, publicans, farm labourers, dry-stone wallers, van drivers, salesmen of one sort or another. We even had our very own famous artist. Michael Stanhope. Well, he's not very fashionable these days. Come with me a minute.'

She struggled out of her deck chair and Annie followed her into the house. Mrs Kettering pointed to a large watercolour that hung over the dark wood mantelpiece. 'That's one of his,' she said. 'He gave it to me as a going-away present. Don't ask me why, but he took a bit of a shine to me. Maybe because I wasn't a bad-looking lass at the time.'

Annie had a passion for art. She stared at Stanhope's painting. 'Is that Hobb's End before the war?'

'Just after war broke out, actually. It was painted from the fairy bridge, looking towards the mill.'

Annie stood back and examined the work carefully. The first thing she noticed was Stanhope's peculiar use of colour. The season was autumn, and he seemed to take the hues and tones hidden deep in stone, fields, hillsides and water and force them out into the open, creating a pattern of purples, blues, browns and greens. It was uncanny, almost surreal in its effect. Next, she noticed the subtly distorted perspective. The mill was there, perched on the rise in the top left corner, and though it *should* dominate the scene, somehow it didn't. The church managed more prominence through its dark and subtly menacing square tower.

The rest of the composition appeared simple and realistic enough: a busy village high-street scene whose people reminded her of Bruegel's. The villagers were shopping, gossiping, pushing prams. A man straddled a roof repairing a chimney; a tall girl stood arranging newspapers in a rack outside the newsagent's shop; a butcher's boy was cycling down the High Street with his basket full of brown-paper packages.

Normal life. But there was something sinister about it. Partly it was the facial expressions. If you looked long enough, you could almost believe that the man on the roof was about to drop a flagstone on some passer-by, and that the butcher's boy was wielding a cleaver ready to chop off someone's head.

The only characters who looked attractive were the children playing in the shallows of the river, splashing one another, paddling. Some of them looked angelic; all of them looked innocent. There was something religious, ecstatic, in the children's aspects, and the link with the water also brought to mind baptism. It was a powerful work.

In the bottom right-hand corner, just above the artist's signature, stood the outbuilding where the skeleton had been found, next to a small cottage. A wooden sign announced the name: BRIDGE COTTAGE.

'What do you think?' Mrs Kettering asked.

'Have you noticed the way everyone looks? As if—'

'As if they were all either hypocrites or sadists? Yes, I have. That's Stanhope's vision. I must say I didn't see Hobb's End like that at all. Would you like to go back out to the garden?'

Annie followed Mrs Kettering outside and sat down again.

'What became of Stanhope?'

'I think he stayed in the village until the bitter end, and then I heard he moved to a small studio in London. But I don't think he managed to find a foothold in the big city art world.'

Annie sat quietly for a moment, taking it all in. 'Bridge Cottage,' she said, 'where we found the skeleton. It looked neglected in the painting.'

'I noticed that, too,' said Mrs Kettering, 'and it made me remember something. I think an old lady lived there. Bit of a recluse, so I can't tell you anything about her. I just remembered, looking at the painting, that some of the children thought she was a witch. I'm sorry I can't be of much help.'

Annie stood up. 'You *have* been helpful. Believe me. Thank you.'

WHEN MATTHEW MET GLORIA that first time, I could feel their immediate attraction like that eerie electric sensation you get before a storm, when you feel jumpy and ill at east for no apparent reason. It scared me; I don't know why.

From that first April meeting, events progressed quickly between them. That very afternoon, Matthew showed her round the village. A few days later they went to the pictures in Harkside and then to the May Day dance there. I was helping out behind the refreshments counter, and I could see the way they danced so close together, the way they looked at one another.

I wasn't at all surprised when Matthew announced that he had invited Gloria to tea one Sunday. Mother was in one of her states, so the preparation all fell to me.

I was listening to *The Brains Trust* after putting the rabbit stew on to simmer, when Gloria popped her head round the door, Matthew right behind her. Mother was still titivating herself in her bedroom.

Gloria's golden hair, parted on the left, tumbled in long wreaths of sausage curls over her shoulders. She was wearing a blue blouse with padded shoulders and puffed sleeves tucked into a simple black skirt with silver buttons down the side. On her lips was just a trace of lipstick. I felt dowdy in my plain old pinafore dress.

'Look what Gloria's brought for us,' Matthew said, holding out a pint of milk and half a dozen eggs. I thanked her.

'Hello, Gwen,' Gloria said. 'I should have known you'd be a *Brains Trust* fan. Tell me, who's your favourite? Joad or Campbell?'

'Joad. He's the most intelligent, the best-read, the most eloquent.'

'Hmm. Probably,' said Gloria, sitting down on the sofa. Matthew sat next to her looking like the proud new owner of . . . well, of something. 'I like Campbell,' she said. 'He's more entertaining.'

'I wouldn't have thought you listened to something like that,' I said, regretting my rudeness almost as soon as the words were out.

Gloria just shrugged. 'I've heard it once or twice.' Then her eyes lit up in that way they had. 'But you're right. If I had a wireless, I'd listen to nothing but music all day long.'

'You don't have a wireless?' Surely everyone had a wireless.

'Mr Kilnsey won't have one in the house. He's rather a strict sort of Methodist, you know. Thinks they're the devil's loudspeaker.'

'Oh, good heavens,' said Matthew, shaking his head.

Gloria nudged him. 'It's true! He really talks like that. Anyway, I don't mind. All I do is work and sleep there.'

'I must go and see to the food,' I said. I put the kettle on to make us all some tea, then I peeled a few potatoes and prepared the carrots and parsnips. We had some onions from the garden and some rhubarb for a pie. If I say so myself, it was a good meal.

The kettle boiled. I made tea and carried it through. With rationing, you had to be sparing, and the tea was a lot weaker than we were used to. With sugar rationed at only a pound a fortnight, and most of that in the rhubarb pie, the three of us had all stopped taking it. I didn't know about Gloria, so I offered her some.

'I gave it up,' she said. 'Actually, I've got a far better use for my sugar ration.' She shook her curls. 'If you mix it with warm water, you can use it as a setting lotion.'

'It must make your head feel terribly sticky,' I said.

She laughed. 'Well, sometimes it's hard to get my hat off, I can tell you. But that can be quite a blessing in the wind.'

At that moment, Mother made her grand entrance. She walked slowly because of her arthritis and her stick tapped against the bare floorboards. She was wearing one of her old flower-patterned frocks, a small, frail-looking figure, a little stooped, with a round, ruddy, pleasant face. It was a kind face, and she was a kind woman.

'What a lovely blouse, my dear,' Mother said after the introductions. 'Did you make it yourself?'

'Yes,' said Gloria. 'I managed to scrounge a bit of parachute silk, then I dyed it. I can make one for you, if you like. I've got a bit more put away up at the farm.'

'Good heavens, my dear, you don't want to waste your time making fancy clothes for an old crippled woman like me. No, what I've got will do to see me out.'

The Brains Trust ended and a special about Jerome Kern came on. Gloria liked that better; she had heard all the songs in her beloved Hollywood musicals. Mother and Gloria got talking about how they both loved Fred Astaire and Ginger Rogers in *Swing Time*.

We turned the wireless off while we ate. 'So, my dear,' said Mother when the stew was served, 'tell us all about yourself.'

'There's not much to tell, really,' Gloria said.

'Oh, come, come. Where are you from?'

'London.'

'Oh, you poor girl. What about your parents?'

'They were both killed in the bombing.'

'Oh dear, I'm so sorry. When was this?'

'Last year. September. I'm all alone now.'

'Nonsense, my dear,' said Mother. 'You've got us.'

I almost choked on my rabbit. 'It's not as if we're adopting her or anything, Mother,' I managed.

'Don't be so rude, Gwen. People have to pull together.'

'Anyway,' Matthew said, 'Gloria's away from all that now, aren't you, darling?'

She looked at him with those big beautiful eyes of hers, adoration just dripping out of them like treacle. 'Yes,' she said. 'I am. And I'm never going back.'

'Is there no one left?'

'No one. I was out visiting a friend a few streets away when the air raid came. I thought my family would go to the underground like we always did in air raids, but they didn't make it in time. My grandparents lived next door, and they were killed, too.'

We were all silent for a few moments, digesting the matter-of-fact horror of what Gloria had just told us.

'What made you decide on a godforsaken place like Hobb's End?' Mother asked.

'That's where they sent me, the Land Army. I was just glad to get away to the countryside.'

After the rhubarb pie, Matthew and Gloria lit cigarettes. Then Matthew cleared his throat and said, 'Mother, I invited Gloria here tonight because, well, we have something to tell you.'

My heart started to thump against my rib cage.

'We want to get married.'

I gaped at Matthew: tall, dashing, handsome, that charming lock of dark brown hair always slipping over his eye, the dimples at each side of his mouth when he smiled, the clear eyes and strong chin. And then I looked at Gloria, saw her radiance.

At that moment, I hated her.

'Ah,' said Mother. 'You do, do you?'

'Very much,' said Gloria, taking Matthew's hand. 'I know we haven't known one another for long, but it's wartime and—'

Mother interrupted her. 'Have you thought, though, that Matthew might be going far away soon?'

'We've thought about that, Mother,' he said. 'Even though I passed the medical, I'll still have my military training to do after the degree, and there's a good chance I'll be able to come home every weekend until after Christmas.'

'Matt will be at Leeds University until July,' Gloria said, 'then he'll go wherever they send him for training. I know it's not perfect. We'd love nothing more than to be together *all* the time, but we know that's not realistic.'

I couldn't believe it; she called him *Matt*. How could she? He had always been Matthew to Mother and me.

'A lot of couples are waiting to marry,' Mother said. 'Until times are less uncertain.'

'But a lot of people are getting married, too,' Matthew argued, 'making the best of the time they have. If anything happens to me in the forces, I'll die a far happier man for having been married to Gloria. Even if it was only for a day.'

Mother glanced at me. 'What do you think about all this, Gwen?'

I swallowed. 'Me? Well, I suppose if it's what they really want to do, then there's nothing we can say to stop them.'

'Good old Gwen,' said Matthew. 'I knew I could depend on you.'

'Where will you live?' Mother demanded. 'It's not that we wouldn't have you, but there's not enough room here, you know.'

'We're going to live in Bridge Cottage,' said Matthew.

Mother frowned. 'What? That run-down hovel by the fairy bridge?'

'Yes. I've talked to Lord Clifford's agent, and he says that the evacuees there are moving out next week. I know it'll need a lot of fixing up, but I'm good with my hands. And it's only five shillings a week.'

'What about children? Have you thought about that, too?'

That sad look came over Gloria's face the way it did sometimes, a dark cloud blocking the sun. 'We haven't planned to have children,' she said. 'Not yet, anyway.' Then she smiled again. 'After the war, though, we'll see. Things will be different then.'

Mother was silent for a moment, then she said, 'You've thought of everything, haven't you?'

Matthew beamed. 'Everything, Mother. Please say you'll give us your blessing. Please!'

Mother looked at Gloria again. 'And you have no living relatives, my dear?'

'None. But you *did* say I've got you, didn't you?'

Mother smiled. 'I did, didn't I? Go on, then, you have my blessing.'

SOME MORNINGS, especially when the weather was good, Vivian Elmsley liked to walk up Rosslyn Hill to Hampstead High Street, take a table outside one of the cafés and linger over her morning coffee to think about the book she was working on; she would sit and scribble a few ideas as she sipped.

Today, though, the book was far from her mind. She opened her newspaper. The item she was looking for appeared in a column on an inside page.

> North Yorkshire Police indicated yesterday that the skeletal remains found under Thornfield Reservoir, on the site of a village called Hobb's End, were those of a female murder victim. Detective Chief Inspector Alan Banks said that the body is that of a woman in her twenties. All indications are that she was stabbed to death. Preliminary information indicates that they are dealing with a twentieth-century crime. Anyone with information is asked to get in touch with the North Yorkshire Police.

So they knew that much already. Her hand trembling slightly, Vivian put the newspaper down.

It was funny, she thought, how over the years she had managed to distance herself from the past: the years with Ronald; her early struggles as a writer after his death; the rejections and humiliations; the flush of first publication; the slow rise to success; the television series. Before Ronald, she had thought her life completely blighted by fate. Instead, it had been far more fulfilling than she could ever have dreamed. But there is always a price to pay, and that was the deep, gnawing guilt that, while it fuelled her imaginative flights of fancy, brought on black moods and sleepless nights she sometimes feared would never end.

Vivian glanced back at her newspaper, folded open at the Hobb's End item, and sighed.

Well, it shouldn't take the police long now, should it? And then what would become of her hard-earned peace?

BANKS STARTED with Brian's university administration office, and ten minutes later, after a few white lies about the importance of the information he was requesting, he had managed to convince the assistant to break her 'strict code of privacy'. On the pad in front of him was Andrew Jones's telephone number in Wimbledon. When he dialled the number, no one picked the phone up, and there was no answering machine.

As soon as he put it down, the phone rang. It was John Webb.

'I've just picked up the stuff we dug up with the Hobb's End skeleton,' he said. 'Dr Williams's lads have given it a good clean.'

'What did you find? Not much, I imagine.'

'Actually, you'd be amazed at the things that *do* survive. I found a few buttons and some metal clips that might have come from a brassiere or a suspender belt. I also found some small leather shoes.'

'So you're saying she was buried in her clothes?'

'Looks like it.'

'Anything else?'

'Yes, some other material, black and heavy. Definitely not clothing. Some sort of curtains, perhaps?'

'Did you find a wedding ring?' he asked.

'I think so. That's what it looks like all right.'

'Any sign of the murder weapon? Most likely some sort of knife. Handbag or a purse? Anything with identification.'

'Sorry, no. Just what I've told you.'

'OK, thanks a lot, John.'

'No problem. I'll have it sent over to you later today.'

Though the health fascists had finally succeeded in banning smoking from every police station in the country, Banks lit a cigarette. He had his own office. With the door closed and the window open, who would know? Banks started to drift into pleasurable fantasies involving Annie Cabbot and her red wellies.

Dream on, he told himself. The truth was that Annie Cabbot

wouldn't have him, and he wouldn't try it anyway. He was too old to go out on dates and worry about whether a good-night kiss would be welcome. He wouldn't know where to begin.

He had had only one sexual encounter since Sandra left, and that had been a disaster. In his cups at a farewell party in the Queen's Arms, Banks had picked up a woman called Karen something-or-other. Karen was tipsy and definitely frisky. Without much preamble, they went back to his place where, later, Banks awoke around four in the morning with a pounding headache, a naked woman wrapped around him and a burning desire to be alone. He never saw her again.

The telephone dragged him out of his depressing memory. It was Geoff Turner, the forensic odontologist.

'Geoff. Any news?'

'Nothing dramatic. Too soon for that. But I was keen to make a start. What I wanted to do first of all was confirm Dr Williams's estimate of her age at the time of death. He's right. The third molars are up—wisdom teeth—but the apexes haven't quite closed yet, nor have the medial sides of the incisal sutures. The third molars don't usually come up until your early twenties. The apexes are usually closed by the age of twenty-five and medials by thirty. Which makes her mid-twenties.'

'Thanks, Geoff. Any idea how long she's been down there?'

'What few fillings there are seem to indicate fairly recent dental work, not later than the fifties, if that's any help. We're not talking top-quality dental work here. There are several missing teeth—pretty clean extractions—and signs of neglect, which may indicate we're dealing with someone who couldn't afford the best treatment. Another possibility is wartime.'

'Really? Why do you say that?'

'Think about it. Most of the good young dentists and doctors were in the forces, and there were only old dodderers left. Poor equipment. Repairs were hard to get done.'

'Right. I didn't think of that. Thanks. I owe you, Geoff.'

'Best of luck, Alan. Talk to you later.'

Banks put down the receiver and leaned back in his chair to think about what he had just heard. If the victim had been between twenty-two and twenty-eight when she was killed, she would probably have been between seventy and eighty had she lived. So her killer might still be alive, then, and so might a witness, or at least someone who *remembered* her.

Chapter Three

As weddings go, Matthew and Gloria's was a relatively small affair. A few family members came from as far away as Eastvale and Richmond, but Gloria had no family, of course, so the rest of the guests were made up of people from the village. Gloria had insisted on inviting Michael Stanhope, as they had become quite close friends. At least he had made the effort to shave, comb his hair and wear a decent, if rather frayed suit.

I must say Gloria looked radiantly beautiful. With her angelic face and earthly figure, she had a natural advantage to start with. She had found her wedding dress on sale at Foster's in Harkside for two pounds ten shillings. It was a simple white affair, both elegant and tasteful. She had made her own veil out of lace.

Wouldn't you know it, clothes rationing came into force the Sunday before the wedding. Luckily, we had all got used to mending and making do by that stage of the war. Cynthia Garmen and I were bridesmaids and we wore matching taffeta dresses made out of some old curtains.

It was June 7, 1941, and a lovely day, with clouds like trails of spilt milk in the sky. The Reverend Graham conducted the service at St Barts and the reception was held in the church hall. Our first American food had just arrived in the shop, so we had Spam for sandwiches, and tinned sausage meat for sausage rolls. We managed to get a keg of watery beer from the Shoulder of Mutton and there was some sweet sherry we had been keeping in our cupboard.

Matthew's friend, Richard Bright, played trumpet with the Victor Pearson Dance Band, so we got at least half the band to come and play for their supper. Gloria and Matthew led off the dancing, of course, and a lump came to my throat as I watched them.

Michael Stanhope remarked on how beautiful he thought Gloria

looked and what a lucky man Matthew was. Betty Warden sat with her nose in the air most of the night, disapproving of everything and everyone, but when she danced with William Goodall she seemed like a different person. Alice Hill was cheerful and talkative as ever, and I rather think she developed a fancy for Eric Poole that night. They certainly danced closely together often enough.

Gloria came up to me at one point. 'This is the happiest day of my life, Gwen,' she said. 'Do you know, just six months ago I thought I would never laugh or dance again. But thanks to you, your mother and, of course, dear Matt . . . Thank you, Gwen, thank you so much.' Then she clasped me to her bosom, giving me a little peck on the cheek. 'I haven't seen you dancing,' she said.

I shook my head. 'I don't. I mean, I can't.'

'I'll teach you,' she said. 'Not right now of course . . .'

She excused herself, and went to talk to Mother, smiling on everyone she passed with those Hardy-heroine eyes of hers.

Matthew and Gloria went to Bridge Cottage for their first night together as man and wife. Whether this was their first *time t*ogether, I have no idea. It may be hard to believe now, but I knew very little of such things back then, being only sixteen at the time. The next day they were going to Scarborough for a three-day honeymoon. After that, it was back to university for Matthew and back to Top Hill Farm for Gloria, though she would live at Bridge Cottage.

I finally excused myself through tiredness and set off home alone. It had been a long, hard day. Back home, I made sure the blackout curtains were drawn tightly, then I went to bed.

It was only when I was on the very edge of sleep and heard the thrumming and droning of the bombers taking off from Rowan Woods RAF Base that I realised that there had been no wedding bells. All the church bells had been silent since 1940 and were only supposed to ring if there was an invasion. I thought that was very sad, and I cried myself to sleep that night.

ANNIE CABBOT PAUSED with the dusty file in her hands when she heard footsteps on the stairs. She was surprised when she saw DCI Banks.

'Inspector Harmond told me you were down here,' Banks said.

Annie gestured around at the musty-smelling, ill-lit basement room. 'Welcome to Central Records,' she said. 'You can see how often we dip into our history around here.'

Banks smiled and walked over to join her. 'Anything yet?'

'Quite a lot. I've been on the phone most of the day, and I was just checking some missing-persons files.'

'And?'

'It's a bit of a confusing period for that sort of thing. Just after the war, so many people coming and going. Anyway, most of the ones who went missing seemed to turn up eventually, either dead or alive, or in the colonies. There are a couple of young women who fit the general description still unaccounted for. I'll follow up on them.'

'Fancy a pint? The Black Swan?'

Annie smiled. 'You took the words right out of my mouth.' What a relief, she thought. She had been in the stifling basement for the best part of the afternoon.

Comfortably ensconced on a padded bench just a few minutes later, pint already half finished, Annie smacked her lips.

'I checked the voters' register first,' she said, 'but the clerk in the council office told me it was frozen at the start of the war. The last person listed for Bridge Cottage is a Miss Violet Croft. I had a bit more luck with the Land Registry. Violet Croft rented the cottage between the 14th of September, 1919, and the 3rd of July, 1940, so she must be the old lady Ruby Kettering remembered. The cottage remained empty until June 1941, when a Mr and Mrs Shackleton took up residence there. It might have been requisitioned for the billeting of evacuees or military personnel in the interim period, but there was no record of that.'

'What happened to Miss Violet Croft?'

Annie flipped over a page in her notebook. 'I dropped by St Jude's next. They've got all the old parish registry records and magazines from St Bart's stored there. Violet Croft, spinster of the parish, died in July 1940 of pneumonia. She was seventy-seven.'

'That lets her out. What about the Shackletons?'

'They were married at St Bart's on the 7th of June, 1941. The husband's name was Matthew Stephen Shackleton, the wife's maiden name Gloria Kathleen Stringer. The witnesses were Gwynneth Shackleton and Cynthia Garmen.'

'Were they Hobb's End residents?'

'Matthew Shackleton was. His family lived at 38 High Street. They ran the newsagent's shop. The bride's listed as being from London, parents deceased.'

'Big place,' Banks muttered. 'How old was she?'

'Nineteen. Born on the 17th of September, 1921.'

'Interesting. That would put her within Dr Williams's age range by the end of the war. Any mention of children?'

'No. I looked through the registry of baptisms, but there's nothing there. Was he certain about that, do you think?'

'He seemed to be. You saw the pitting for yourself. Do you know what? I'm beginning to get a vision of St Catherine's House looming large in your future.'

Annie groaned. Checking birth, marriage and death certificates was one of the most boring jobs a detective could get. The only positive aspect was that you got to go to London.

'Any luck with the education authorities?' Banks asked.

'No. They said they lost the Hobb's End records, or misplaced them. Same with the doctors and the dentist. I think we can say goodbye to that line of inquiry.'

'Pity. What does your instinct tell you, Annie?'

Annie was surprised. No senior officer had ever asked for her *feelings* before, for her *feminine intuition*. Banks was certainly different. 'Well, sir,' she said, 'for a start, I don't think it's a killing by a stranger. It *looks* domestic. Like that bloke who killed his wife and sailed off to Canada.'

'Dr Crippen? He buried his wife under the cellar.'

'Cellar. Outbuilding. Same difference.'

'All right, I take your point. Conclusion?'

'Victim: Gloria Shackleton. Killer: husband, or someone else who knew her.'

'Motive?'

'God knows. Jealousy, sex, money?'

'*Blackout curtains.*' Banks slapped his palm on the table.

'Come again, sir?'

'Blackout curtains. John Webb said they found some heavy black material with the body. It makes sense now. The body was wrapped in blackout curtains, Annie. And Geoff Turner mentioned possible wartime dental work. I think we're dealing with a wartime crime.'

'Brilliant, Holmes.'

'Elementary. Anyway, Gloria Shackleton fits the bill as victim. Before we go any further, let's find out all we can about her. She hasn't shown up as missing?'

'Not in any records I've seen.'

'Right.' Banks looked at his watch. 'How about something to eat? I'm getting hungry. Are there any decent restaurants in Harkside?'

Annie paused for a moment, then gave in to a little surge of devil-may-care excitement that tingled through her and said, 'Well, sir, there's always my place.'

AFTER THE HONEYMOON, Gloria continued to report for work at the farm, and at weekends she was at Bridge Cottage, looking fresh and beautiful, ready for Matthew's arrival. Matthew passed his engineering degree, and started his military training at Catterick, which wasn't too far away. Most days I was busy with the shop.

We managed to get to the pictures in Harkside together a few times. Gloria just loved films.

Sometimes we accepted a lift with some of the RAF boys from Rowan Woods, and we even became quite friendly with a couple of Canadian airmen attached to the RAF: Mark, from Toronto, and Stephen, from Winnipeg. Mark was the more handsome one, and I could tell he liked Gloria by the way he looked at her. Gloria seemed amused by it all. Sometimes we let them take us to the pictures and they were both very well behaved.

For Gloria's twentieth birthday, in September, I took her to Brunton's Café on Long Hill, where we gorged ourselves on grilled sausage with mashed potatoes and braised butter beans, followed by jam roll and custard. Matthew couldn't be with us because it was a weekday. After tea, we went to the Lyceum to see *Ziegfeld Girl*, starring Jimmy Stewart and Lana Turner. It was so memorable that the next day I couldn't remember a single melody. It was Gloria's choice, of course. Unfortunately, our tastes couldn't have been more different. Gloria liked empty-headed Hollywood musicals and romantic comedies with beautiful stars and handsome leading men, whereas I preferred something with a bit of meat on its bones.

Sometimes Alice, Cynthia and Betty came to the pictures with us, even Michael Stanhope on occasion. While he often delighted us with his wicked critical commentary on the way home, he disappointed me in leaning more towards Gloria's sort of film.

Matthew and Gloria tried to furnish Bridge Cottage as best they could. You had to scrounge for the simplest of things, like curtain rods and coat hooks. They went to auctions some weekends, bought a wardrobe here, a dresser there, and bit by bit managed to make a home out of Bridge Cottage. Gloria's pride and joy was the radiogram they bought from the Coopers after their son, John, was killed when HMS *Prince of Wales* was sunk just before Christmas. His mum and dad couldn't bear to keep it after he died.

Gloria honoured her promise to give me dancing lessons and I spent an hour or so over at Bridge Cottage each weekend while Matthew read the newspaper after dinner. I learned the waltz, the quickstep and the foxtrot. I actually tried out my skills at a Bonfire Night dance in the Harkside Mechanics Institute. I did very well at dancing, and that worked wonders for my confidence.

By Christmas, Matthew had almost finished his training, and there was talk of a posting, but he said there wasn't much hope of a shopkeeper's son getting a commission.

It was also that Christmas when I got my first real inkling of Gloria's problems with men.

ANNIE'S PLACE turned out to be a squat, narrow terraced cottage at the centre of a labyrinth. Banks left his car parked by the green and they walked through so many twisting narrow streets and ginnels that he was lost within seconds.

'Why do I keep thinking I should have left a piece of thread attached to the Black Swan?' he said as he followed her.

Annie cast a glance over her shoulder and smiled. 'Like Theseus, you mean? I hope you don't think I'm the Minotaur?'

Banks's mythology was a bit rusty, but he remembered an ancient vase he had seen on a school trip to the British Museum. It depicted Ariadne outside the Labyrinth holding one end of the thread and Theseus at its centre killing the Minotaur.

Annie opened a high wooden gate in a stone wall, led him through a small flagged yard and in the back door.

'Where do you park?' Banks asked.

Annie laughed. 'A long way away. Look, it's tiny, there's not much of a view and very little light. But it's mine. Well, it will be when I've paid off the mortgage.'

She led him through to the living room. It was small but cosy, and she had decorated much of it in whites, lemons and creams because of the lack of outside light. As a result, the room seemed airy and cheerful. There was just enough space for a small white three-piece suite, a TV, mini-stereo and a small bookcase under the window. Several miniature watercolours hung on the walls. Local scenes, mostly. There was also one oil portrait of a young woman with flowing Pre-Raphaelite hair and laughing eyes.

Annie put her hand to her head and swept back her hair. 'Look, I feel really grubby after being down in that basement. I'm going up for a quick shower first, then I'll start dinner. Make yourself at home. There's beer in the fridge.' Then she left the room. Banks heard stairs creak as she walked upstairs.

This woman was an enigma, he thought. She had a DCI, her boss, as a guest in her house, yet nothing in her behaviour indicated a deferential relationship. He heard the shower start.

First, he did what he always did when left alone in a new room; he nosed around. Curiosity was part of his nature. He crouched down and checked the CD titles in the cabinet under the stereo. It was an odd collection: Gregorian chants, Don Cherry's *Eternal Now* and several 'ambient' pieces by Brian Eno. There was also an extensive blues collection. Next to these stood a few pop and folk titles. The books mainly centred around Eastern philosophy.

Then Banks wandered into the kitchen, opened the fridge and took out a bottle of Black Sheep beer. He found an opener and a pint glass in one of the cupboards. Carefully, he poured out the beer, then he took a sip and went back into the living room. He took *Eternal Now* from its case and put it in the CD player. He had heard of Don Cherry, a jazz trumpeter, but didn't actually know his work.

Before the first track had finished, Annie breezed into the room exuding freshly scrubbed warmth.

'I never took you for a Don Cherry fan,' she said, a wicked grin on her face.

'Life is full of surprises. I like it.'

'I'll start dinner now.' She disappeared into the kitchen. 'You can keep me company,' she called out over her shoulder.

Banks carried his beer through. He sat down at the kitchen table. Annie was bending over, pulling vegetables out of the fridge.

'Pasta OK?' she asked, half turning her head.

'Great. It's a long time since I've had any home cooking. Mostly these days it's been either pub grub or something quick and easy from Marks and Sparks.'

'Ah, the lonely eater's friends.'

Annie filled a large pan with water, added a little oil, then set it on the gas ring. She washed and chopped mushrooms, shallots, garlic and courgettes. There was a certain economic grace to her movements; she seemed to possess a natural, centred quality that put Banks at ease. Soon the oil was hot in the frying pan and she was dropping the vegetables in. When they were done, she added tinned tomatoes and herbs. About the time Banks finished his beer, Annie announced that dinner was ready and delivered two steaming plates to the table. Banks grated Parmesan onto the pasta and tucked in. He complimented Annie.

'See,' she said. 'It's not all salads and tofu. You learn to be more inventive in the kitchen when you're a vegetarian.'

'I can tell.'

'Wine?'

'Please.'

Annie brought over a bottle of Bulgarian Merlot, poured herself a glass and one for Banks. 'You know, I'd really like to find out more about this Hobb's End artist, Michael Stanhope. He *was* living in Hobb's End during the war. Maybe he knew the Shackleton woman. There may be other paintings. They might tell us something.'

'They might,' Banks agreed. 'Though I'm not sure how far art could be trusted as evidence.'

Annie smiled. 'Not technically, perhaps. But artists often distort reality to reveal the truth about it. The artist's reality is as valid as any other. Perhaps more so because an artist struggles to see more deeply, to illuminate. Stanhope obviously perceived something odd about Hobb's End, something that went below the surface, beyond the superficial ideas of village life. He saw something *evil* there and maybe something redemptive about the children.'

'Isn't that a bit far-fetched? Maybe it was just because there was a war coming.'

'I'm not trying to make out he was a visionary. Just that he really *looked* and maybe he saw something other people could not see that might be useful to us.'

Banks sipped some wine. 'You seem to know a lot about the subject.'

'My father's an artist.'

'Is he well known?'

'Not really. In some circles, perhaps.' She smiled crookedly. 'Ray will never go down in history as one of the greats.'

'What about your mother?'

Annie was silent for a few moments. 'She died,' she said at last. 'When I was six. I don't really remember her very well.'

'That's sad. I'm sorry.'

'More wine?'

'Please. That oil portrait in the living room, is it your mother?'

Annie nodded.

'Your father painted it?'

'Yes.'

'She was a beautiful woman. You look a lot like her.'

It was almost dark outside now. Annie hadn't put on any lights, so Banks couldn't see her expression.

'Where did you grow up?' he asked.

'St Ives.'

'Nice place. I've been there on holiday a couple of times.'

'I don't get down as often as I should. In the sixties it became something of an artists' colony. Over the years my father's done all kinds of odd jobs to support his art. Now he paints local landscapes and sells them to tourists. He's quite successful at it.'

'He brought you up alone?'

Annie pushed her hair back. 'Well, not really. We lived in a sort of artists' colony on an old farm just outside town, so there were always lots of other people around. My extended family, you might call them. Ray's been living with Jasmine for nearly twenty years now.'

'It sounds like a strange set-up.'

'Only to someone who hasn't experienced it. Some of the locals thought we were having orgies every night, doing drugs, the usual stuff. Actually, though there always seemed to be some pot around, they couldn't have been further from the truth. On the whole it was a pretty good environment to grow up in.'

'What made you join the police?'

'The village bobby took my virginity.'

'Seriously.'

Annie laughed. 'It's true. He did. His name was Rob. He came up to see us once, looking for someone who'd passed through. He was good-looking. I was seventeen. He noticed me. It seemed a suitable act of rebellion. I'd had enough of that lifestyle by then. Too much talk and not enough done. And Rob seemed solid, dependable, more sure of himself and what he believed in.'

'Was he?'

'Yes. We went out until I went to Exeter University. Then he turned up there a year or so later as a DC. He introduced me to some of his friends and we sort of started going out again. I suppose they found me a bit weird. I was into yoga and meditation. I didn't really fit in anywhere. I don't know why, but being a detective sounded exciting. *Different*. It was a bit impulsive, I'll admit.'

Banks wanted to ask her why she was in a dead-end place like Harkside, but he sensed that this wasn't the moment. 'What happened to Rob?'

'He got killed during an armed drugs bust three years later. His gun jammed.'

'I'm sorry.'

Annie fanned her hand in front of her face. 'Ooh, I'm hot. Listen to me go on. I haven't talked to anyone like this in ages.'

'I wouldn't mind a cigarette. Would you like to stand outside with me? Cool down a bit, if it's possible?'

'OK.'

They went out into the back yard. It was a warm night, though there were signs of a breeze. Annie stood beside him. He lit up, inhaled and blew out a plume of dark smoke.

'I'm like you in a lot of ways,' she said.

'What do you mean?'

'Well, how much have you told me about your past? You're a loner, like me. I don't just mean now, because you're . . .'

'Because my wife left me?'

'Right. I mean I think you've got a lonely, isolated nature. It colours the way you see the world, the detachment you feel. I think I'm the same.'

It was what Sandra had said when they had their final argument. There was something in him that always stood apart, that she couldn't reach and he wouldn't offer. It wasn't just the job and its demands, but something deeper: a central core of loneliness. He had always been on the outside, an observer, even as a child. As Annie said, it was a part of his nature, and he didn't think he could change it if he tried.

'Maybe you're right,' he said.

Banks dropped his cigarette and trod on the red ember. Suddenly a chill gust of wind rustled the distant trees and passed through the yard. Annie shivered. Banks put his arm around her and moved her gently towards him. She let her head rest on his shoulder.

'Oh dear,' she said. 'I don't know if this is a good idea.'

'If it's the rank thing that's bothering you—'

'No. No. I don't give a damn about that. It's just that . . . I've had some bad experiences with men. I mean . . . Oh, shit, why is this so difficult?' Banks kept silent. Annie sighed deeply. 'I've been celibate,' she said. 'By choice. For nearly two years now.'

'I don't want to pressure you,' Banks said.

'Don't worry. I wouldn't let you. I make my own choices.'

'I'll never find my way out of this labyrinth alone.'

'I'd lead you,' Annie said, facing him and smiling. 'If I really wanted you to go.' She rested her hand on his chest. His heart beat loudly. Surely she could hear it, feel it? 'There are a lot of reasons for not taking this any further, you know,' she went on. 'I've heard you're a bad lot. A womaniser.'

'Not true.'

They looked at one another for a few moments. Annie bit her lip, shivered again and said, 'Oh, hell.'

Banks leaned forward and kissed her. Her lips yielded and her body moulded itself to his.

Matthew and Gloria had decided to have a party on Christmas Eve. The guests started to arrive at Bridge Cottage at about seven o'clock, including airmen from the base, some with their girlfriends. Alice's Eric was away in North Africa by then, but Betty's William hadn't passed his medical, so they would only let him in the Home Guard. Michael Stanhope came dressed in his usual artistic 'costume', but he did bring two bottles of gin and some wine, which made him most welcome indeed. Mark and Stephen had also contributed a bottle of Canadian Club whisky.

Matthew and Gloria had decorated the tiny front room as best they could, with balloons, concertina streamers and fairy lights over the mantelpiece. There was a Victor Sylvester concert on the radio that night, and soon people were dancing close together in the cramped space. Cynthia and Johnny Marsden hogged the sofa and kissed one another. Gloria drank too much Canadian Club and then switched to gin. She wasn't loud or falling down or anything, but there was a sort of glaze to her eyes and a slight wobble in her step.

I got distracted by an RAF radio operator who first dragged me under the mistletoe and gave me a kiss that tasted of tinned sardines, then proceeded to explain radiolocation to me. I should have told him I was a German spy.

I realised I hadn't seen Gloria for a while and wondered if she was sick or something. I needed to go to the toilet anyway, so I disengaged myself from the radiolocation lecture. It was cold and dark outside, so I put my coat over my shoulders, picked up a torch with its tissue-filtered light and headed out into the back yard.

Bridge Cottage had two outbuildings; one was the toilet and the other was used for storage. As I made my way down the flagstones to the toilet, suddenly I heard sounds nearby. I paused, then I heard a grunt and a muffled voice calling out. The sounds were coming from behind the toilet. Puzzled, I tiptoed over and pointed my torch.

What I saw made my skin tingle. Gloria was pinned to the wall by Mark, the Canadian airman. Her dress was bunched around her waist, and the white flesh of her bare thighs above the stocking-tops stood out in the darkness. Mark was crushed forwards into her, one hand over her mouth, the other fumbling at his waist.

Gloria was calling out in a muffled voice, 'No, please, no!' over and over again, trying to struggle against him. When he saw my

light, he swore at me and took off round the front of the house.

Gloria leaned back against the wall, gasping and sobbing, her hair and clothes in disarray. Then she straightened her dress, leaned forward and was sick.

I didn't know what to do. I wasn't even sure what sort of scene I had witnessed—except that there was something very wrong about it. All I knew was that Gloria looked hurt, upset and in pain. So I did what came naturally; I opened my arms and she fell into them.

THERE WAS ENOUGH LIGHT through the thin curtains for Banks to see Annie breathing softly beside him. She lay on her side, curled away from him, hands clasped in front. Gently, Banks touched her. Annie stirred a little but still she didn't wake.

He rolled onto his back and closed his eyes. His only fear last night had been that he would feel the same way he had when he slept with Karen. He should have known better. He should have known this would be different. Afterwards, Annie had rested in the crook of his arm and he knew then that he wouldn't wake with a burning desire to be alone.

Just for a moment he wondered if this was a trap Riddle had set for him. Were there hidden cameras in the bedroom? Were the two of them plotting Banks's final downfall? Then, as quick as it came, the paranoia was gone. Jimmy Riddle clearly didn't know DS Cabbot, otherwise he wouldn't have sent Banks within twenty miles of her.

Annie stirred and Banks ran his hand slowly all the way from her hip to her shoulder.

'Mmm . . .' she murmured. 'Good morning.'

'Good morning.'

Banks hooked his arm over her side and rested his palm on her stomach, easing her closer. He kissed the soft flesh between her shoulder and neck, then slid his hand up to cup her small breast. Annie sighed and Banks turned her gently towards him.

'THE OTHER NIGHT,' said Gloria the next time I saw her alone. 'At the Christmas party. I want to thank you. If you hadn't come along, I don't know what would have happened. I just don't want you to think it was something it wasn't.'

'I don't know what I think it was,' I said. I felt embarrassed, her talking to me like this.

'He followed me out there,' she said. 'I didn't mean to, but I suppose I might have given him some encouragement. He called me a tease, said I'd been leading him on all night. Things just got a bit out of hand, that's all.'

'What do you mean?'

'Oh, I don't know. Men. It seems like they just can't stop themselves. They're so strong. And sometimes it's easier just to give in.'

'Is that what you were doing? Giving in?'

'No. I was struggling, but Mark had his hand over my mouth. I love Matt, Gwen, I didn't want to cause a fuss, get Matt upset. Can we just forget about it?' Gloria pleaded.

I nodded. 'That's probably for the best.'

She gave me a hug. 'Good. And we're still friends, Gwen?'

'Of course.'

AFTER BANKS HAD GONE, Annie did her usual twenty minutes of meditation, followed by a few yoga exercises and a shower. As she dried herself, she realised how good she felt.

She hoped Banks wasn't the kind who felt a moral obligation to fall in love just because he slept with a woman. She wanted to see more of him, yes; she wanted to sleep with him again, yes; but beyond that, she didn't know what she wanted. Still, maybe it would be nice if he did fall a little bit in love with her. Just a little bit.

For the moment, another beautiful summer's day beckoned, and it was a great luxury not to have to make any more serious choice other than whether to do her washing or go shopping in Harrogate.

Before going anywhere, though, she picked up the phone and dialled a number she knew by heart.

It rang six times before a man's voice answered.

'Ray?'

'Annie? How are you doing, my love? We're having a bit of a party.'

Annie could hear laughter and music in the background. 'But it's only ten o'clock in the morning,' she said.

'Is it? Oh, well, you know how it goes. *Carpe diem* and all that.'

'Dad, when are you going to grow up? Haven't you realised yet that we're in the nineties, not the sixties? One day the police will come and bust the lot of you.'

'Police? They're not interested in a couple of teeny-weeny joints, are they? Anyway, how is my little WPC Plod? Getting any, lately?'

'Dad!' Annie felt herself blushing.

'All right. Sorry. Just showing a bit of fatherly concern, that's all. Anyway, wonderful as it is to talk to you, it's not like you to phone before discount time. Anything I can help you with? Like me to beat up a couple of suspects for you?'

'As a matter of fact,' Annie said, 'there is something you might be able to help me with. The artist, Michael Stanhope.'

'Stanhope . . . Sounds familiar. Wait a minute . . . Yes, I remember. Let me see. He didn't live up to his early promise. Died some time in the sixties, I think. Why?'

'I saw a painting of his in connection with a case I'm working on.'

'What was it? The painting.'

Annie described it to him. 'Yes, that'd be Stanhope. He had a reputation for Bruegelesque village scenes. Touch of Lowry thrown in for good measure. That was his problem, you know: too derivative and never developed a style of his own.'

'Do you know where I can find out more about him? Is there a book?'

'I don't think so. He wasn't that important. Most of his stuff will be in private collections, maybe spread around the galleries, too. Why don't you try Leeds? They're bound to have a few Stanhopes, what with him being local and all.'

'Good idea,' Annie said. 'I'll do that.'

AND FRIENDS WE REMAINED. We saw the New Year in together, linked arms and sang 'Auld Lang Syne'. Hong Kong had fallen to the Japanese on Christmas Day and the fighting in North Africa and in Russia went on as bitterly as ever.

Though I often thought about what I had witnessed, I had no way of knowing how culpable Gloria had been. So I did the best I could to put the whole episode out of my mind.

On January 15, 1942, Sergeant Matthew Shackleton shipped out.

He didn't know where he was headed, but we all assumed he would be going to North Africa to fight with the Eighth Army.

Imagine our surprise when Gloria got a letter from Matthew in Ceylon, then another from Calcutta, India. I could have kicked myself for not guessing earlier. They didn't need bridges and roads in the desert, of course, but they needed them in the jungles of the Far East.

ANNIE PARKED north of Leeds city centre and walked down New Briggate to The Headrow. The place was busy, pavements jammed with shoppers. She put on her sunglasses and set off through the crowds towards Cookridge Street. A little research had revealed that Leeds City Art Gallery had in its collection several works by Michael Stanhope.

Once inside, she picked up a guidebook at the reception area. The Stanhopes were on the second floor. Four of them. She started up the broad stone staircase.

When she found the Stanhopes, she was at first disappointed. Two of them were rather dull landscapes, not of Hobb's End, but other Dales scenes. The third showed a distant view of Hobb's End in its hollow, smoke drifting from chimneys, the bright vermilions and purples of sunset splashed across the sky. A fine effect, but it told Annie nothing she didn't know.

The fourth painting, though, was a revelation.

Titled *Reclining Nude*, according to the catalogue, the painting reminded Annie of Goya's *The Naked Maja*. The woman reclined on a bed in much the same pose, propped on a pillow, hands behind her head, looking directly at the painter with a highly charged erotic challenge in her expression. Also, like the *Maja*'s, her round breasts were widely spaced and her legs bent a little, awkwardly placed as her lower half twisted slightly towards the viewer. There were differences, though. Stanhope's model had golden-blonde hair rather than black, her large eyes were a striking blue, her lips fuller and redder.

But there was more to Stanhope's vision. If you looked very closely, you could see images of tanks, aeroplanes, armies on the march, explosions and swastikas in the background. Eroticism and weapons of mass destruction. Make of it what you would.

Annie glanced at the note on the wall beside the painting, then she stepped back with a gasp.

There it was, plain as day, below *Reclining Nude*. A subtitle: *Gloria, Autumn 1944*.

ON MONDAY MORNING, Banks looked again at the postcard reproduction of *Reclining Nude: Gloria, Autumn 1944* that lay on his desk. It was an uncanny and disconcerting experience to see an artist's impression of the flesh that had probably once clothed the filth-covered bones they had found last week.

Thrilled by her discovery, Annie had phoned him late on Saturday afternoon. They met for dinner at Cockett's Hotel, in Hawes, with every intention of going their separate ways later, both having agreed that they shouldn't rush things. After the second bottle of wine, though, instead of leaving, they took a room and woke to Sunday-morning church bells. After a leisurely breakfast, they left, agreeing to restrict their trysts to weekends.

As he looked at Gloria's pose—beautiful, erotic, sensual, playful, but also challenging, mocking, as if she shared some sort of secret with the artist—he felt that on this case he was needed as much as he'd ever been. All the petty duties and details of a policeman's job aside, Banks's obsession was with bringing down as many bullies as possible. When the victims were dead, of course, he couldn't defend them, but he could damn well find out what had happened to them and bring the bullies to justice. He was convinced that Gloria Shackleton was the victim they had found buried at Hobb's End, and he wanted to know what had happened to her.

A call from Dr Glendenning, the Home Office pathologist, cut into his thoughts.

'Ah, Banks,' he said. 'I'm glad I caught you in. You're very lucky I happened to be in Leeds, you know. Otherwise you could have whistled for your post-mortem. There are plenty of fresh cadavers craving my expert attention.'

'I'm sure there are. My apologies. What have you got?'

'Nothing much to add to what Dr Williams told you, I'm afraid. She was stabbed viciously, fifteen or sixteen times, as far as I can tell. It's not possible to say what killed her, though judging from the angles and positions of the knife wounds, the blade would almost certainly have pierced several vital organs.'

'Did you find evidence of any other injury?'

'Patience, laddie. That's what I'm getting to, if you'll slow down and give me the chance. I found possible, and I stress *possible*, signs of manual strangulation.'

'Strangulation?'

'That's what I said. And stop echoing me. If I needed a bloody parrot I'd buy one. I'm going by the hyoid bones in the throat. Now, these are very fragile bones, almost always broken during manual strangulation, but the damage could have occurred over time, due to other causes. The weight of all that earth and water, for example. I must say, though, the skeleton was in remarkable condition considering where it's been for so long.'

'Would that make it more probable than possible?'

Glendenning sighed theatrically. 'All right, shall we say it's certainly not impossible, and even quite *likely*, that the poor woman was strangled.'

'Before she was stabbed.'

'It would seem very unlikely to me that her killer felt any need to strangle her *after* he had done this. I'd say the strangulation came first and then, for whatever reason, the stabbing. That kind of thing is statistically more common, too.'

'So why the stabbing? To make sure she was dead?'

'I doubt it. Whoever did it got carried away with killing. Either that or he knew exactly what he was doing and he enjoyed himself.'

'Right,' said Banks, scrawling away on the pad he'd pulled in front of him. 'Thanks very much, Doc.'

ALL THROUGH FEBRUARY 1942, day after day, I followed the news reports. I read about the estimated 60,000 British taken prisoner in Singapore, and the fighting near the Sittang River, from where Matthew wrote Gloria another letter, telling her not to worry. Then, on March 8, we heard about the fall of Rangoon.

Our morale at home was pretty low. One week you couldn't get fish for love or money; the next it was poultry. The civilian petrol ration was cut out completely in March. In April, the Germans gave up all pretence of bombing military and industrial targets and

started bombing cities of architectural beauty, such as York, which was getting very close to home.

I wrote to Matthew every day, which was probably more often than Gloria did. She was never much of a letter writer. Matthew didn't write back that often, but when he did he would always assure us he was well. Mostly, he complained about the monsoons and the humid jungle heat. For a long time we didn't even know if he had been in battle. Once, though, he wrote: 'Long stretches of boredom relieved only by the occasional brief skirmish.'

That September, *Pride and Prejudice,* with Laurence Olivier and Greer Garson, finally came to the Lyceum. Gloria had just had a tooth extracted by old Granville, the dentist, after suffering toothache for several days. As usual, Granville did more damage than good, and poor Gloria had been bleeding for over a day. She was just beginning to feel a little better and I managed to persuade her to come to the pictures with me. It made a nice change from all the comedies and musicals she had been dragging me to see lately.

It was a beautiful autumn evening tinged with smoky green and golden light. As we walked across the fields that night, I could see the purple heather darkening on the distant moor-tops to the west and could smell clean, hay-scented air.

Despite the war, I felt deeply content at that moment. Yet as we came down towards the fairy bridge in the gathering darkness, I felt a chilling shudder of apprehension, as if a goose had stepped over my grave, as Mother would say.

As the weeks passed, I tried to dismiss the feeling, but it had a way of creeping back. There was plenty to rejoice about, I told myself: Matthew continued to write regularly; the Red Army seemed to be making gains at Stalingrad; and the tide had turned in North Africa.

But after the victory at El Alamein that November, when the church bells rang for the first time in years, all I could do was cry because Matthew had had no bells at his wedding.

'FIRST OFF,' Annie told Banks over the phone later that day, 'I can find no official record of Gloria Shackleton at all after the wedding notice in 1941. There's no missing-persons report in our files and no death notice anywhere.'

'OK. Go on.'

‘Well, I was able to dig up a bit more about her life at Hobb’s End, mostly from the parish magazine. In the May 1941 issue, she’s welcomed to the parish as a member of the Women’s Land Army, assigned to work at Top Hill Farm, owned by a Mr Frederick Kilnsey and his wife, Edith. They had one son called Joseph, who was called up. That’s why they got Gloria. Joseph didn’t come back. Killed at El Alamein. By then, Gloria was living at Bridge Cottage. Unfortunately, the parish magazine stopped publication early in 1942. Paper shortage.’

‘Pity. Go on.’

‘That’s about it, really. Matthew Shackleton’s younger sister Gwynneth—who witnessed the marriage—was still around in March 1942. Wrote a piece on growing your own onions, in fact.’

‘How fascinating. What about Matthew?’

‘The last time he was mentioned he was shipping overseas. Didn’t say where. Secret, I suppose.’

‘Any idea where any of these people moved to when they cleared out of Hobb’s End?’

‘No. But I rang Ruby Kettering. She’s remembered that she knows two people who lived in Hobb’s End during the war. There’s Betty Goodall, who lives in Edinburgh, and Alice Poole in Scarborough.’

‘OK. Which do you fancy: Edinburgh or Scarborough?’

‘Doesn’t matter to me.’

‘I’ll toss for it. Heads or tails?’

‘How can I trust you over the telephone?’

‘Trust me. Heads or tails?’

‘This is crazy. Heads.’

Banks came back on. ‘It was heads. Your choice.’

‘I’ll take Scarborough.’

‘OK. If I get an early enough start I can be up to Edinburgh and back by early evening. I’d like to get something on tonight’s news, first. I want to put Gloria’s name out, see if anything comes back.’

‘So Jimmy Riddle thinks he’s dropped you in it with this one, then?’ said DS Hatchley after swallowing his first bite of toasted tea cake.

‘To put it succinctly, yes,’ said Banks.

They were sitting in the Golden Grill, just across the street from Eastvale Divisional HQ. Outside, Market Street was packed with tourists, cameras round their necks. Like sheep up on the unfenced moorland roads, they strayed all over the narrow street.

Once they had given their orders to the bustling waitress, Banks told Hatchley about the skeleton. By the time he had finished, their order had arrived.

Banks knew his sergeant had a reputation as an idle sod and a thug. His appearance didn't help. Hatchley was big, slow-moving and bulky, and he usually looked as if he had just been dragged through a hedge backwards. But it had always been Banks's experience that once Hatchley got his teeth into something, he was a stubborn and dogged copper.

'Anyway, what I'd like you to do is take PC Bridges and go down to London, to St Catherine's House, tomorrow. Here's a list of information I'd like.' Banks passed over a sheet of paper.

Hatchley glanced at it. 'Can't I take WPC Sexton instead?'

Banks grinned. 'And you a married man? I'm ashamed of you, Jim. Before you go, could you put out a nationwide request for information on similar crimes in the same time period? It's an old crime, but there's a chance someone might have something similar on the books.'

'You think this was part of a series?'

'I don't know, Jim, but what Dr Glendenning told me about the MO made me think I shouldn't overlook that possibility.'

The door opened and WPC Sexton walked over to them. DS Hatchley nudged Banks and pointed. 'Here she is. The belle of Eastvale Divisional.'

'Piss off, Sarge,' she said, then turned to Banks. 'Sir, we just got an urgent message from a DS Cabbot in Harkside. She wants you to get down there as soon as you can. She said a lad named Adam Kelly has something he wants to tell you.'

THE TELEGRAM, in its unmistakable orange cover, came to the shop, for some reason. I remember the date; it was Palm Sunday, April 18, 1943. Gloria was working that day so, heart thumping, I had to run up to Top Hill Farm.

I found Gloria collecting eggs in the chicken shack.

'What are you doing here, Gwen?' she said.

Panting, I handed over the telegram to her. She read it, her face turned ashen and she sagged back against the wall. The chickens squawked and the sheet of paper fluttered to the dirt floor. 'Oh, no,' she said. 'No.' Then her whole body started to tremble. I wanted to go to her, but somehow I knew that I must let the first pangs of grief shake her and rip through her alone.

MRS KELLY ANSWERED the door and asked them in. Banks could sense the tension immediately. The aftermath of a scolding; it was a familiar childhood sensation of his, and the scoldings had usually been dished out by his mother.

'He won't say owt,' Mrs Kelly said. She was a plain, harried-looking woman in her early thirties, old before her time, with limp hair and a drawn face. 'I challenged him on it when he came home from school and he ran up to his room. He won't come down.'

'Challenged him on what, Mrs Kelly?' Banks asked.

'What he stole from that . . . that there skeleton. I left it where I found it when I were cleaning his room. Anyone would think I haven't brought him up right. It's not easy when you're on your own.'

'Calm down, Mrs Kelly,' Annie said, stepping forward. 'Nobody's blaming you for anything. Or Adam. We just want to get to the bottom of it, that's all.'

'May I go up and talk to him?' Banks asked.

'Suit yourself. You'll get nowt out of him. Left at the top of the stairs.'

Banks glanced at Annie, who tried to settle Mrs Kelly in an armchair, then he made his way up. He knocked first on Adam's door and, getting no response, opened it and stuck his head round. 'Adam?' he said. 'It's Mr Banks. Remember me?'

Adam lay on his side on the single bed. He turned slowly, and said, 'I didn't mean nothing, honest I didn't. I don't want to go to jail.'

'Nobody's going to take you to jail, Adam. Why don't you just calm down and tell me what happened. Can I come in?'

Adam sat up on the bed. His eyes were red with crying. 'Suppose so,' he said.

Banks sat on the edge of the bed. Posters of muscular sword-and-sorcery heroes hung on the walls. A small computer sat on a desk.

'Why don't you tell me about it?' he asked.

'I thought it were magic,' Adam said. 'The Talisman. That's why I went there. Hobb's End. It's a magic place. It were destroyed in a battle between good and evil, but there's still magic buried there.'

'You found something that day, when you fell, didn't you?'

Adam nodded.

'Will you show it to me?'

The boy reached under his pillow and pulled out a small round object. He hesitated, then passed it to Banks. It was a metal button, by the look of it. Corroded, but clearly a button of some sort.

'Where did you find this, Adam?'

'It fell into my hand, honest.'

Banks turned away to hide his smile. 'All right,' he said. 'What were you doing when it fell into your hand?'

'Pulling the hand out.'

'It was in the skeleton's hand?'

'Must've been, mustn't it?'

'Why didn't you tell us about it sooner?'

'I thought it were the Talisman. It's not easy to get. You have to pass through the veil to the Seventh Level.'

Banks hadn't a clue what the boy was talking about. Not that it mattered. 'You did well,' he said. 'But you should have passed this on to me the first time I came to see you. It's not a talisman, it's just an old button.'

Adam seemed disappointed. 'Is it important?'

'I don't know yet. It might be.'

'Who was it? Do you know? The skeleton?'

'A young woman.' He held out the button on his palm. 'This might help us find out who killed her.' Banks stood up. 'You can come down now. Nobody's going to do you any harm.'

'But my mum—'

'She was just upset, that's all. Come on downstairs.'

Adam's mother was in the kitchen making tea, and Annie was leaning against the counter talking to her.

'Oh, so you've decided to join us, have you, you little devil?' said Mrs Kelly.

'Sorry, Mum.'

She ruffled his hair. 'Just don't do owt like that again.'

VIVIAN ELMSLEY SAT DOWN with her gin and tonic to watch the news that evening. The drinks were becoming more frequent, she had noticed, since her memories had started disturbing her.

Tonight, the news shook her to the core.

Towards the end of the broadcast, the scene shifted to Hobb's End, where crime-scene searchers were still digging up the ruins.

'Today,' the reporter began, 'in a further bizarre twist to a story we have been covering in the north of England, police investigating some skeletal remains are almost certain they have established the identity of the victim. Detective Chief Inspector Alan Banks, who is heading the investigation, talked with our northern office.'

The camera settled on a dark-haired man with intense blue eyes.

'Can you tell us how this discovery was made?' the reporter asked.

'Yes.' Banks looked straight into the camera as he spoke. 'When we discovered the identity of the people living in the cottage during the Second World War,' he began, 'we found that one of them, a woman called Gloria Shackleton, hasn't shown up on any postwar records. Of course, there could be a number of reasons for this, but one thing we are forced to consider is that she hasn't shown up because she's dead.'

'How long have the woman's remains been buried?'

'It's hard to be accurate, but we're estimating between the early to mid-forties.'

'That's a long time ago. Is there any way the public can help?'

'Yes, there is.' The next moment, the screen was filled with the head and shoulders of a woman. Surely it couldn't be? But there was no mistaking who it was: *Gloria*.

Vivian gasped and clutched her chest.

It looked like part of a painting. Gloria must have been lying down as she posed. Michael Stanhope? It looked like his style.

In the background, Banks's voice went on, 'If anyone recognises this woman, who we think lived in London between 1921 and 1941 and in Hobb's End after that, would they please get in touch with the North Yorkshire Police.' He gave out a phone number.

All Vivian could see was Gloria's face: Stanhope's vision of Gloria's face, with that cunning blend of naiveté and wantonness, that come-hither smile and its promise of secret delights. Then she thought, with a tremor of fear: if they had already discovered Gloria, how long would it take them to discover *her*?

Chapter Four

'It only said he's *missing*,' Gloria insisted over two months later at the height of the summer of 1943. We were standing by one of Mr Kilnsey's dry-stone walls and looking out over the gold-green hills. She thrust the most recent Ministry letter towards me. 'See: "Missing during severe fighting east of the Irrawaddy River in Burma."'

What had kept us going the most since we heard the news of Matthew's disappearance was our attempt to get as much information as we possibly could about what had happened to him. First we had written letters, then we had even telephoned the Ministry. But the most we could get out of the man on the phone was that the area in which Matthew had disappeared was in the hands of the Japanese. Matthew was not among confirmed casualties. He might have been killed, taken prisoner. It was impossible to get anything further out of him. Gloria had been brooding over what to do next.

'I think we should go down to Whitehall,' she said. 'Get some answers.'

For the rest of that month I tried to talk her out of the London trip, but she was adamant. Even Michael Stanhope said it would be a waste of time: government bureaucrats would tell us nothing.

I had never been to London, and the prospect scared me stiff.

It was finally arranged for September. Gloria decided it would be best if we went and returned by night train. That way she would only have to rearrange her one and a half days off for midweek. Cynthia Garmen said she would look after Mother and the shop. Mother gave Gloria some of her clothes coupons to use if we had time to visit the big shops. Though she accepted them gratefully, for once clothes were the last thing on Gloria's mind.

IT WAS ABOUT TEN O'CLOCK when the road crested the hill and Banks could see Edinburgh spread out in all its hazy glory: the stepped rows of tenements; the dark Gothic spire of the Scott Monument, the hump of Arthur's Seat; the castle on its crag; the glimmer of the sea beyond.

Betty Goodall, lived just off Dalkeith Road, not far from the city centre. She had given him precise directions on the telephone, and after only a couple of wrong turns he found the narrow street of tall tenements.

Mrs Goodall answered Banks's ring promptly and led him into a high-ceilinged living room that smelt of lavender. She was a short, stout woman and her recently permed hair was almost white. Its waves looked frozen, Margaret Thatcher style.

She bade him sit in a sturdy damask armchair, its arms and back covered by white lace antimacassars.

'Well, then, you're here. Tea?'

'Please.'

She disappeared into the kitchen. Banks surveyed the room. It was a nondescript sort of place: clean and tidy, but not much character. A few framed photographs stood on the sideboard, but none of them showed Hobb's End.

Mrs Goodall walked back into the room slowly, carrying a china tea set on a silver tray. She set it down on a doily on the low table in front of the sofa, then sat down.

'We'll just let it mash a few minutes. Now,' she said, hands clasped on her lap, 'let us begin. You mentioned Hobb's End on the telephone. What do you wish to know?'

'Do you remember Gloria Shackleton?' Banks asked. 'She lived in Bridge Cottage during the war.'

Mrs Goodall looked as if she had just swallowed a mouthful of vinegar. 'Of course,' she said. 'Dreadful girl.'

'Oh? In what way?'

'Not to put too fine a point on it, Chief Inspector, the girl was a brazen hussy. I knew it the first moment I set eyes on her in church. She was still called Gloria Stringer then.'

'Was she religious?'

'No true Christian woman would go about flaunting herself the way she did.'

'Why did she go to church, then?'

'Because the Shackletons went, of course. She had her feet firmly under their kitchen table.'

'She was from London originally, wasn't she? Did she ever say anything about her background?'

'Not to me, though I vaguely remember someone told me her parents were killed in the Blitz.'

Mrs Goodall sat up, back erect, and poured the tea. The cups were tiny, fragile bone-china things with a handle he couldn't possibly get a finger through.

'Of course,' she went on, 'one hoped that over time she would make attempts to fit in, to alter her manner according to the standards of village society, but she made no attempt at all.'

'Did you know her well?'

'Chief Inspector, does she sound like the kind of person whose company I would cultivate?'

'Did you have any dealings with Gloria at all?'

Mrs Goodall nodded. 'Indeed I did. It fell to me to advise her that her behaviour was unacceptable, as was the way she looked.'

'Looked?'

'Yes. The sort of clothes she wore, the way she sashayed about, the way she wore her hair. It was not ladylike.'

'You say it *fell* to you? On what authority? Was there strong general feeling against her?'

'In my capacity as a member of the Church of England.'

'I see. How did Gloria react when you rebuked her?'

Mrs Goodall flushed at the memory. 'I pointed out that it might do her much good, morally and socially, were she to become active in the Women's Institute and the Missionary Society. She called me an interfering busybody and indicated that there was only one missionary position she was interested in, and it was *not* the Church's. And she used language I would not expect from the mouth of the lowest mill girl.'

'She married Matthew Shackleton, didn't she?'

Mrs Goodall sucked in her breath with an audible hiss. 'Yes. Matthew was an exceptional boy. I expected far better of him than that. It wasn't long after they were married he was sent abroad. He went missing in action, poor Matthew, some time in 1943.

Captured by the Japanese.' She gave a shudder. 'I presume he died.'

'You lost touch?'

She fiddled with her wedding ring. 'Yes. My husband, William, was posted to Scotland early in 1944. I accompanied him and we didn't have anything more to do with Hobb's End.'

'Do you know if Gloria had affairs?'

Mrs Goodall sniffed. 'Almost certainly.'

'Who with?'

She paused, then uttered just one word. 'Soldiers.'

'What soldiers?'

'This was wartime, Chief Inspector. There were soldiers everywhere. Not all of them British, either.' For the first time in their conversation, Mrs Goodall let a small smile slip. 'Oversexed,' she said, 'overpaid and over here.'

'Americans?'

'Yes. The RAF handed Rowan Woods over to the American air force. They often used to come and drink in the village pubs, or attend our dances at the church hall. And I needn't tell you about the opportunities for immorality and indiscretion that a wide area of wooded land like Rowan Woods had to offer, need I?'

Banks wondered if she would take a positive answer as an indication of personal experience. He decided not to risk it. 'Did Gloria have anyone in particular?' he asked.

'I have no first-hand knowledge. I kept my distance from them. According to Cynthia Garmen, she had more than one. Not that Cynthia was one to talk. She married one of them, didn't she? Went off to live in Pennsylvania.'

'So there was no one serious for Gloria?'

'Oh, I've no doubt her liaisons were every bit as serious as such a woman was capable of. A *married* woman.'

'But you said she thought her husband was dead.'

'Missing, *presumed* dead. It's not quite the same.' Mrs Goodall remained silent for a few moments, then said, 'May I ask why you are asking me about the Shackleton girl after all these years?'

'Don't you watch the news? Read newspapers?'

'I prefer historical biography.'

Banks told her about the discovery of the body they believed to be Gloria's. Mrs Goodall paled. 'I don't like to speak ill of the dead,' she muttered. 'You should have told me sooner.'

'Would that have changed what you said?'

'Probably not. I have always considered telling the truth to be an important virtue. I can tell you, though, that Gloria Shackleton was alive and well when we left Hobb's End in May 1944.'

'Thank you,' said Banks. 'That helps us narrow things down a bit. Do you know if she had any enemies?'

'Nobody who would do what you have just described. Many people, like myself, disapproved of her. But that's quite a different thing. Given Gloria's wayward nature, don't you think you should be looking at this as a *crime passionnel*?'

'Perhaps.' Banks shifted in his chair. 'What about Michael Stanhope?' he asked.

She raised her eyebrows. 'There's another one. Debauched, perverted. Birds of a feather, him and Gloria Shackleton.'

'I wonder if you knew anything about a nude painting of Gloria?'

'I can hardly say it surprises me, but no. It was *not* public knowledge in Hobb's End while I was there.'

'Do you think she might have had an affair with Stanhope?'

'I can't say. I wouldn't rule it out. They did spend a lot of time together.'

'Did Gloria and Matthew have any children? There were certain indications in the post-mortem.'

'Not that I ever knew of. It's hard to hide such things in a small village. Of course, she could have had a child after we left in 1944.'

'It's possible. Or perhaps she gave birth *before* she arrived in Hobb's End.'

'But . . . but that means . . . Surely that would indicate she was already married?'

'Just one more sin to add to her list,' said Banks. 'But it wasn't necessarily so. I imagine even back then, in the good old days, the odd child was born on the wrong side of the blanket.'

Mrs Goodall's lips tightened. 'I don't appreciate your sarcasm, Chief Inspector, or your coarseness.'

'I'm sorry, Mrs Goodall. I don't mean to be sarcastic, really, but I'm trying to get to the bottom of a particularly nasty murder here. I believe the victim deserves my best efforts.'

'Of course. I stand corrected. Gloria Shackleton could not possibly have deserved what you say happened to her.'

'Did you know Matthew's sister, Gwynneth?'

'Gwen? Oh, yes. Gwen was always rather the quiet one, head buried in a book.'

'Do you know what became of her? Is she still alive?'

'I'm afraid we lost touch when William and I came to Scotland.'

'Were she and Gloria close?'

'Well, they were always off to dances together in Harkside, or to the pictures. But they were as different as chalk and cheese. There was some talk about Gloria leading Gwen astray. Gwen was a few years younger, an impressionable girl.'

'What did she look like?'

'Gwen? She was rather a plain girl, apart from her eyes. Remarkable eyes, almost oriental the way they slanted. And she was tall. Tall and awkward. A gangly sort of girl.'

'What about Matthew?'

'A dashing, handsome fellow. Very mature.' Again, she allowed a little smile to flit across her hard-set features. 'If I hadn't met my William, well . . . who knows?'

Banks stood up. 'You've been a great help.'

'If there's anything else I can help you with, please don't hesitate to telephone.'

GLORIA AND I TOOK the night train from Leeds, where the platform was crowded with young soldiers. We felt ourselves jostled along like corks in a fast-flowing river and finally managed to get ourselves more or less pushed onto seats in a cramped compartment.

Everyone was crushed too closely together for sleep to be possible. I couldn't even read. The blinds were drawn tight and the compartment was lit by one ghostly blue pinpoint of light.

We talked for a while with two young soldiers. Then people started to fall silent. For me it was a matter of gritting my teeth and enduring the long journey, the unexplained delays, the jerking stops and starts. Gloria dozed off after a while and her head slid slowly sideways until she was resting her cheek on my shoulder.

It was in the last hour or so that I caught my first sight of street after street of bombed-out London terraces. Rosebay willowherb

and Oxford ragwort grew from the rubble, pushing between the cracks in the bombed masonry and brickwork. Some houses were split open like a cross-section. You could see wallpaper, framed paintings and photographs on the walls, a bed half-hanging over the jagged remains of the floor. I'm not sure that I had any real grasp of the full extent of the war's devastation until then.

It was after ten o'clock in the morning when we arrived at King's Cross and I was starving. Gloria wanted to head straight for Whitehall, but I persuaded her to stop and we found a Lyons, where we managed to get a rasher of bacon and an egg.

After breakfast, we walked back into the street. The whole place had a shabby, worn and slightly defeated air about it. I saw my first wounded soldiers, sad-looking men with bandaged heads, missing limbs, eye patches, some on crutches or with their arms in slings. Everybody looked pinched and pale, after years of rationing, bombing and uncertainty.

Gloria was in her element. We took a bus and got off on a broad street flanked with tall buildings where our search began. I felt like a small child dragged along by its mother as Gloria took me from building to building. Finally, Gloria found a minor clerk who did seem to know a little more about the war in the Far East than anyone else would admit to. And he appeared to take a shine to Gloria.

He was a tidy little man in a pinstripe suit, with grey hair parted at the centre and a neat, trim moustache. He glanced at his watch, before suggesting he might spare us ten minutes if we cared to accompany him to the teahouse on the corner.

We bought tea at the counter, and Gloria started to pump the poor fellow for information.

'What are the chances that Matthew might still be alive?'

The man, who told us his name was Arthur Winchester, hemmed and hawed a bit, then measured his words carefully. 'I'm afraid I can't really answer that question,' he said. 'As I told you, I have no knowledge of individual cases, merely a little general knowledge of the situation in the East.'

'All right,' Gloria went on, undaunted, 'tell me about what happened at Irrawaddy.'

Arthur Winchester paused and sipped some tea. 'Burma,' he said, 'as you probably know, stands between India and China, and it would be of inestimable value if our forces could reopen the Burma Road and clear the way to China, which could then be used as a direct base for operations against Japan. This is general knowledge.'

'Not to me it isn't.' Gloria lit a Craven A. 'Go on,' she prompted, blowing out a long plume of smoke.

'To put things simply, since Burma fell, we have been trying to get it back. One of the offensives was the Chindit Operation, launched in February. They began east of the Irrawaddy, a river in central Burma. While they were there, the Japanese launched a major offensive on the Arakan Front and the British had to withdraw. The Chindits, the Allied fighters who operated behind Japanese lines, were trapped, cut off, and began to filter back in some disarray.' He looked at Gloria. 'This, no doubt, is why no one has been able to give you any specific information about your husband.'

'But we're still trying to get Burma back?'

'Oh, yes. It's of great strategic importance.'

'So there's still a chance that someone might find Matthew? When the British win back Burma?'

'I wouldn't get your hopes up, my dear. A long time might pass before that happens.'

'How do you know all this?' Gloria asked.

Arthur Winchester inclined his head modestly. 'I don't know very much, I'm afraid. But before the war I was a history teacher. The Far East has always interested me.'

'So you don't really have anything to tell us?' Gloria said.

'Well, any excuse to take tea with a pretty lady will do for me, if you don't mind my saying so.'

Gloria got to her feet in a fury. Arthur Winchester grabbed hold of her sleeve meekly. 'I say, my dear, I'm sorry. Poor taste. I really didn't mean to offend you. A compliment, that's all.'

Gloria sat down again, slowly, a hard, suspicious look in her eyes, and said, 'Can you tell us anything at all, Mr Winchester?'

'All I can tell you, my dear,' he went on gravely, 'is that during the retreat, many of the wounded had to be left behind enemy lines. They were left with a little money and a weapon.'

Gloria had turned pale. I found myself twisting the fabric of my dress in my fist over my lap until my knuckles turned white.

'And what if that is what happened to Matthew?'

Arthur Winchester paused. 'Well,' he said, 'the Japanese don't like taking wounded prisoners. It would depend how badly wounded he was, of course—whether he could work.'

'So they might have simply murdered him?'

'I'm saying it's possible. Or . . .' He looked away. 'As I said, the wounded were left behind with a weapon.'

It took a second or two for what he was getting at to sink in. 'You mean Matthew might have committed suicide?' I said.

'If capture was inevitable, and if he was badly hurt, then I'd say, yes, it's a possibility.' His tone brightened a little. 'But this is all pure conjecture, you understand. Maybe he was simply captured and he's in the relative safety of a prison camp. The main problem is that our lines of communication are very poor. Even the Red Cross has great difficulties getting its parcels delivered and getting information. The Japanese are notoriously difficult to deal with.'

'So he may be a prisoner of war and nobody has bothered to let anyone know? Is that what you're telling us?'

'That is a distinct possibility. Yes. But . . .' He paused. 'Well,' he said. 'I don't want to upset you, but I'd say it's best to hope he's dead. It's best that way.' He paused again. 'Look. It's wartime. Things are very different. You have to let go of the past. Your husband is probably dead. Or, if he isn't, he might as well be. Nothing will ever be the same when it's done. All over the city people are living as if there's no tomorrow. How long are you staying in London?'

Gloria looked at him suspiciously. 'Until tonight. Why?'

'I know a place. Very discreet. Perhaps I could—'

Gloria got to her feet so fast she bumped the table and the remains of her tea spilt onto Arthur Winchester's lap. But he didn't stop around to mop it up. Instead, he bolted for the door saying, 'Good Lord, is that the time? I must dash.'

Gloria glared after him for a moment, then touched up her curls and sat down again.

We dawdled over our tea. Gloria smoked another cigarette and gazed out through the steamed-up window. 'What did he mean, "It's best that way"?'

'I don't know,' I said. 'I suppose he meant to say that the Japanese

don't treat their prisoners as well as we do. It sounded to me as if he was saying that Matthew would be better off dead.'

ANNIE PARKED IN ONE of the hilly streets at the back of Scarborough Castle, and went looking for Alice Poole's cottage. The sky was bright blue, with only a few wisps of white cloud borne on the sea breeze.

She found the cottage easily enough. It was in a high, quiet part of town, away from the pubs and shopping centres crowded with holidaymakers. From the garden she could see a wedge of the North Sea far below, steely grey-blue today, dotted with small boats. Flocks of gulls gathered, squealing, above a shoal of fish.

The woman who answered the door was tall, with thin, wispy hair like candyfloss. She was wearing a long, loose purple dress with gold embroidery round the neck and dangling gold earrings of linked hoops. A pair of black horn-rimmed glasses hung on a chain round her neck.

'Come in, love.' She led the way into a bright, cluttered room. 'Can I offer you coffee?' she asked, having settled Annie in an armchair. 'I usually have elevenses around this time.'

Annie smiled. 'Thanks, Mrs Poole.'

'Alice. Call me Alice. And why don't you have a look through this.'

She handed Annie a thick leatherbound photograph album and headed for the kitchen. Most of the deckle-edged black and white photographs were family groups, but several were village scenes. There were also a couple of pictures of the church and mill.

Alice Poole came back holding a mug of coffee in each hand and a KitKat between her teeth. 'A little indulgence of mine,' she said when she had freed her hands. 'Would you like one?'

'No,' said Annie. 'No, that's fine.' She accepted her coffee.

'You've come about poor Gloria, then?'

'You've heard?'

'Oh, yes. Your boss was on telly last night. How horrible. Have you got any suspects yet?'

'Not really,' said Annie. 'It's very difficult, what with it all being so long ago.'

'You don't say. I was seventy-five last birthday. Look, this is

Gloria.' Alice turned to a photograph of four girls standing in front of a Jeep and pointed to a petite blonde with long curls, a narrow waist and a provocative smile. Underneath was written 'July 1944'. 'This one's Gwen, her sister-in-law.' Gwen was the tallest. She wasn't smiling and had half turned away, as if shy about her looks. 'And this one here is Cynthia Garmen. That one's me.' Alice had been a svelte blonde, by the look of her. Also in the photograph, standing in the Jeep, were four young men in uniform.

'Who are they?' Annie asked.

'Americans. That one's Charlie, and that's Brad. We saw quite a lot of them. I don't remember the names of the other two.'

'I'd like to make a copy of that photo, if you don't mind.'

'Not at all.' Alice detached the photograph from its corners. 'Please take care of it, though.'

'I promise.' Annie slipped it in her briefcase. 'You knew Gloria well?' she went on.

'Quite well. She married Matthew Shackleton, as you probably know, and while he was away at war, Gloria and Gwen, Matthew's sister, became inseparable. But quite often the gang of us would do something together.'

'What was she like?'

'Gloria?' Alice unwrapped her KitKat and took a bite. 'Well, I'd say she was a good sort. Cheerful. Fun to be with. Kind. Generous. She'd give you the shirt off her back.'

'Did she tell you anything about her past?'

'All she said was that she lost her family in the Blitz. It must have been very painful for her, so I just thought, if she doesn't want to talk about it, then that's all right with me. She did sometimes seem very distracted. She had deep, quiet, sad moods that would just come on her out of nowhere. But not often.'

'Did she have any enemies?'

'Quite a few people disapproved of her. She went in the pubs by herself, and she smoked in the street. I know that's nothing now, love, but back then . . . Well, to some people it meant you were nigh on a prostitute.' She shook her head slowly. 'And Gloria was far too cheeky and flighty for some people. Betty Goodall, in particular, could never take to her. Betty always was a bit too High Church, if you ask me.'

'Do you know whether Gloria actually *did* anything to merit such disapproval, or was it simply her personality?'

'Oh dear. You want me to tell tales out of school?'

Annie laughed. 'Not if you don't want to. But it *is* a long time ago, and it might help us find her killer.'

'Oh, I know, love. I know.' Alice waved her hand. 'Just let me get my cigarettes.' She got up and brought her handbag over, fiddled for a packet of Dunhill and lit one with a slim gold lighter. 'Now then, dearie, where was I?'

'I wanted to know if Gloria had affairs, slept around.'

'Certainly no more than a lot of others did then. She was a bit of a flirt, but that doesn't mean anything, does it? I may have been naive, but I think there was more smoke than fire. Most of the time.'

'What did you think of Matthew?'

'Oh, he was nice enough, handsome and charming, and one had to feel sorry for what happened to him later.'

'What happened?'

'Killed by the Japanese. Over in Burma.'

'How did Gloria take his death?'

'She was heartbroken. Devastated. I was worried about her. Gwen said she'd be OK in a while, but then Gwen didn't look too good herself, either. Very close, they were, her and Matthew. Anyway, when Gloria started to go out again a few months later, she was more devil-may-care, you know, the way some people get when they feel they've nothing left to lose.' She took a drag on her cigarette.

'When did Gloria form her relationship with Michael Stanhope, the artist?'

'Oh, he'd always been around. He was at their wedding. Gloria used to drink with him in the Shoulder of Mutton. They were both outsiders, freethinkers. On some level, they understood one another.'

'Did you know Stanhope?'

'Just to say hello to. He was an eccentric. Always wearing that floppy hat of his. And the cane. Very affected. There was no mistaking that he was an *Artist*. But I think he was harmless enough. Anyway, he wouldn't have had anything to do with Gloria. He was a homosexual, dearie. Queer as a three-pound note, as we used to say.'

'I see. Was Gloria involved with anyone in particular after her husband's death?' Annie asked.

'She had a bit of a fling with a Yank called Billy Joe something or other. She got a bit of a reputation for hanging around with American airmen, disappearing into the woods late at night, that sort of thing.' Alice winked.

'Do you think there was anything in it?'

'I'd be surprised if there wasn't. I think she was lonely. We met a lot of them, Betty, Cynthia, Gloria, Gwen and me. We'd go to dances, mostly at the base or in Harkside. Most of the local lads were at war, except those unfit for service or in reserved occupations and they just hung out in the Shoulder of Mutton and complained. The Americans were different. They talked differently, spoke about places we'd only seen at the pictures. They were exotic. Exciting. They also had all sorts of things we hadn't been able to get—nylons, cigarettes and that stuff. We were friendly with PX, the chap who ran their stores, and he used to get us all sorts of stuff. Gloria in particular. She was definitely his favourite. She was like a beautiful, exotic butterfly; she attracted every man who met her.'

'This PX, what was his real name?'

'Sorry, love, I don't know if I ever knew. We just called him PX.'

'Was there anyone else in particular?'

'After Billy Joe, she developed a real soft spot for Brad. She didn't want anything serious but Brad was head over heels.'

'Do you remember his second name?'

'Sorry, love.'

'How long did they go out together?'

'There you've got me. They were still seeing each other when I left at Christmas 1944. My Eric got wounded. Nothing serious, but it got him an early discharge. The doctor recommended a bit of sea air, so we came here, fell in love with the place and ended up staying.'

'Did Gloria ever mention anything about having a baby?'

Alice looked puzzled. 'No, not to me. I'm not even sure she liked children. Wait a minute, though . . . Once, after Matthew had gone, when I was crossing the fairy bridge I noticed a bloke turn up with a little lad in tow. They went in to see Gloria. I heard voices raised.'

'Who was he, do you know?'

'Sorry, dearie, I've no idea.'

'Did you ever ask Gloria about him?'

'Yes. She went all quiet on me. She did that sometimes. All she would say was that it was relations from down south. You don't think . . .?'

'I don't know,' said Annie. 'Did they ever come back?'

'Not that I ever heard of.'

'And what happened to Gwen and Gloria after you'd left?'

'I don't know. I never saw or heard of Gloria again. I sent her a postcard, must have been March or April of 1945, telling her we were going to stay in Scarborough. She never replied. You lose touch with a lot of people over the course of your life, I've found. It was the same with Gwen. But we did have some good times together.'

'Well, Alice,' Annie said, 'I think that's all for now. You've been very helpful.'

'It's so nice of you to say so, dearie. I must admit, I've enjoyed having a good chinwag. It's been years since I thought about all that stuff.'

ON HIS WAY BACK from Edinburgh, Banks called in at the station. He found about twenty telephone messages in response to Monday evening's television news appearance. He spent an hour or so returning calls, but most people simply wanted to relive wartime memories, and all he found out was that someone thought the Shackletons had moved to Leeds after V-E Day.

There was also a message from John Webb, who said he had cleaned up the button. It was made of brass, probably, and had a raised pattern on the front, possibly reminiscent of wings. Clearly, he added, given the time period under consideration, the armed forces came to mind, perhaps the RAF.

When Banks had finished at the station, he phoned Annie and asked if she would mind coming up to Gratly. He would take her out to the Dog and Gun in Helmthorpe for dinner and hope to

God there was something vegetarian on the menu. Then he went home and took a long shower. Next he tried phoning Brian again. Still no luck. He'd have to try again the next day.

When Annie arrived, she first showed him the photograph of Gloria and her friends. Then, after a lightning tour of his house, they walked to Helmthorpe in the hazy evening light, sharing the information each had learned that day.

It was early September now, and the nights were drawing in fast. When they got to the High Street, the sun was already low in the west, a red ball glowing like an ember through the gathering haze. Sounds of laughter and music came from the open pub doors.

They managed to find a table in the beer garden out at the back. Between the trees, the dying sunlight streaked the river shallows blood-orange and crimson. Annie sat down while Banks went to buy a couple of pints and order food. Luckily, Annie said she wasn't very hungry and a cheese-and-pickle sandwich would do her fine.

'Cheers,' Banks said when he came back. 'So who have we got now, then?' he asked. 'Now we've discovered that Matthew was killed before Gloria was.'

Annie leaned back and stretched out her long legs. 'What about the boyfriend?' she suggested. 'The American.'

'Brad? As her killer? Why?'

'Why not? I get the impression that Gloria exerted considerable power over men. Alice thought he was more keen on Gloria than she was on him. Maybe she tried to shake him loose and he wouldn't go.'

'We definitely need to find out more about the Americans in Hobb's End,' said Banks. 'The American Embassy might be able to point you in the right direction.'

'I notice the subtle pronoun usage there: "you".'

Banks laughed. 'Rank has its privileges. I'll be trying to get more information on Matthew Shackleton. Besides, you're so good at it.'

Annie pulled a face and flicked some beer at him.

Their food arrived, and they both ate in silence for a while.

'What about Michael Stanhope?' Banks suggested.

'What possible motive could he have had? They were friends.'

'Inordinate desire? If he was powerfully attracted to Gloria, if she wouldn't have anything to do with him sexually, then painting her in the nude might have inflamed him beyond all reason.'

Annie raised her eyebrows. 'You'd be surprised how dispassionate an artist can be. The impression I get is that a lot of villagers projected negative feelings onto Gloria. I think she was basically a decent woman, but her good looks and her free and easy attitude gave her no end of problems, especially with men. Eventually someone went over the top.'

'You sound as if you know what you're talking about.'

Annie turned away and stared at the dark river. It had only been a teasing, offhand remark, but Banks felt as if he had trespassed on some private reserve, set her hackles up. They still had to be careful with one another, he realised.

After a pause, Annie went on, 'Besides, Alice also said he was gay.'

'She couldn't know that for certain. He could have been bisexual. Anyway, there's one obvious flaw with the Stanhope theory. If anything happened between them, it would be more likely to have happened at his studio. That's where she was naked in front of him. If he killed her, I don't think he would have risked carrying the body all the way back to Bridge Cottage. He would have found somewhere closer to dispose of her. Another drink?'

'Better not,' Annie said. 'One's my limit when I'm driving.'

Banks paused a moment, his voice lost somewhere deep in his chest. 'You don't *have* to drive home,' he said finally.

Annie smiled and put her hand on his arm. Her touch set his pulse going faster. 'No, but I think I should, with it being a week night and all. Besides, we agreed, didn't we?'

'Can't blame a bloke for trying. Mind if I have one?'

She laughed. 'Course not.'

Banks went inside. He hadn't expected Annie to rise to his offer, but he was disappointed. Surely there was room for a little spontaneity now and then? He wondered if he would ever be able to figure out this relationship business.

He bought himself another pint and went back outside. Annie wasn't much more than a silhouette now—and a beautiful one to his eyes, with her graceful neck and strong profile—staring at the river in that peculiarly relaxed and centred way she had.

He sat down and broke the spell. 'What about this mysterious stranger and the child who turned up? Gloria's family was killed in the Blitz, but she told Alice that the man and boy who visited her were relations.'

'I know. It does seem odd, doesn't it?'

'If she ran off and left a husband or boyfriend stuck with her kid, that might be someone else with reason to be angry with her. He could have tracked her down later and killed her.'

'Yes, but maybe whoever it was didn't feel *stuck* with the kid. Maybe he loved the boy,' Annie said. 'I'd also like to know what happened to the sister-in-law, Gwynneth.'

'Maybe she's dead. Do you see her as a suspect?'

Annie frowned. 'Something could have happened between them.'

'There are a lot of things we don't know about what happened.'

'You realise we might never know who killed her, don't you?'

Banks finished his drink and nodded. 'If that's what it comes down to, we make out a final report based on all the evidence we've collected and point at the most likely solution.'

'How do you think you'll feel about that?'

'What do you mean?'

'It's become important to you, hasn't it? I'm not saying I don't care. I do. But for you it's something else. You have a sort of compulsion.'

Banks lit a cigarette. 'Somebody has to give a damn.'

'That sounds melodramatic.'

Banks tried to frame his nebulous thoughts. 'I know what Gloria Shackleton looked like. I've got some idea of her character, who her friends were, the things she liked to do.' He tapped the side of his head. 'She's real enough for me in there, where it counts. Somebody took all that away from her. Somebody strangled her, then stabbed her fifteen or sixteen times, and buried her in an outbuilding.'

'Murders happen all the time. What's so different about this one?'

Banks shook his head. 'I don't know. Partly, it's the war. Somehow the idea of this murder being committed while all that carnage was going on makes it seem even more of a travesty, and as far as we can tell, nobody reported Gloria missing. It looks as if nobody cared. Somebody has to. I seem to be good at it, overburdened with compassion, a natural.' Banks smiled. 'Am I making sense?'

Annie brushed his sleeve with her fingers. 'I care, too,' she said. 'Maybe not in the same way, but I do.'

Banks looked into her eyes. He could tell she meant what she was saying. He nodded. 'I know you do. Home?'

They walked out into the street, much quieter now night had fallen. Luckily, there was a moon, for there was no other illumination on the narrow, flagged footpath that curved round the steep banks of Gratly Beck up the daleside to the village itself.

Through the narrow stile at the other end, the pavement was broader, and Annie slipped her arm through his. They crossed the stone bridge, walked along the lane and stood at his front door.

'Coffee?' Banks asked.

Annie smiled. 'No, but I'll have a cold drink.'

He left her in the front room rummaging through his compact-disc collection while he went to the fridge.

He took out a carton of orange juice and poured them each a glass. An old Etta James CD started playing in the living room. Funky and fiery. He hadn't played it in years.

'You've got a hell of a CD collection,' Annie said. 'It's a wonder you can ever decide what to play.'

'It *is* a problem sometimes. Depends on the mood.'

Soon Etta was belting out 'Jump Into My Fire'.

'Sure you won't have a nightcap?' Banks asked when Annie had finished her orange juice.

'No. I told you, I've got to drive back.'

'It's a pity,' said Banks. 'I was hoping you might change your mind.'

'Come to Mama' was playing now, and the music's rhythmic, slow-moving sensuality was getting to him. He had to keep telling himself that Annie was a detective sergeant, someone he was working with on a case, and he shouldn't even be thinking like this. But the problem was that Annie Cabbot didn't seem like any detective sergeant he had ever come across before.

'Well,' said Annie, smiling. 'I didn't say I had to go just yet, did

I?' Then she stood up and pulled her T-shirt slowly over her head. With her head tilted to one side, she smiled, held out her hand and said, 'Come to Mama.'

THERE ARE GIANT redwood trees in California, they say, that can grow another layer round the dead and blackened wood if they ever burn in a forest fire. Matthew's disappearance burned out my core like that and while, over time, I did grow another skin over it, there was part of me inside that was always black and dead. There still is.

Of course, life went on. It always does. Gloria threw herself into her work at the farm. In time, we laughed and smiled again.

In October, *Gone With the Wind* finally came to Harkside, and Gloria and Mr Stanhope practically dragged me to see it. As it turned out, I enjoyed the film, and Gloria, needless to say, was potty about Clark Gable.

In September we had heard that the Rowan Woods Aerodrome had been closed and the RAF had gone somewhere else. One of the ground crew told me that the runways at Rowan Woods had to be converted to be able to handle four-engined bombers. A crew of labourers, mostly Irish, came in. Over the next couple of months, they brought in tons of cement, gravel and Tarmac to bring the runways up to standard. Shortly before Christmas, Rowan Woods became the new home to the United States Eighth Air Force's 448th Bomber Group.

The Yanks had arrived.

THOUGH WORRY and fear had gnawed away at her since the TV broadcast, Vivian Elmsley tried to live a normal life: wandering up to Hampstead in the morning; sitting in her study for the day, whether she wrote anything worth keeping or not; talking to her agent and publisher; answering correspondence. All the while waiting for that knock on the door, wondering what she would say.

When it came, though, the shock was in a form she hadn't in the least expected.

That Tuesday night, the phone rang just as she was dropping off. When she picked up the receiver, all she heard was silence.

'Who is it?' she asked.

More silence.

She was just about to hang up when a voice she didn't recognise whispered, 'Gwen? Gwen Shackleton?'

'My name's Vivian Elmsley. There must be some mistake.'

'There's no mistake. I know who you are. Do you know who I am?'

'I don't know what you're talking about.'

'You will. Soon.'

Then the caller hung up.

Chapter Five

Christmas 1943. It was a gloomy, chill and moonless night when the 448th held their first dance at Rowan Woods. Gloria, Cynthia, Alice and I walked there together through the woods. We wore court shoes and carried our dance shoes because they were far too precious and flimsy to walk in.

Alice did a little dance. 'Ooh, just think of it, all those Yanks with money to throw away. They get paid much more than our boys, you know.'

'Don't you try to tell yourself they won't want *something* in return, Alice Poole,' said Gloria. 'And don't you forget your poor Eric away fighting for his country.'

We were all a bit quiet after that. I couldn't help thinking of Matthew. A fox or a badger suddenly flashed across the path and broke the silence. We were still excited, and we giggled like silly schoolgirls the rest of the way.

We had taken special care with our appearance—even me, who was generally not overly concerned about such superficial matters. We all had our best dresses on. Gloria, of course, looked gorgeous in her black velvet V-neck dress with the puffed sleeves and wide, padded shoulders. I was in a utility dress I had bought in London.

Cynthia was going for the Dorothy Lamour look—a black page-boy hairdo and a lot of make-up. Alice was in her Marlene Dietrich period: plucked eyebrows pencilled in a high arch, wavy blonde hair parted in the centre and hanging down to her shoulders. She was

wearing a burgundy dress with long, tight sleeves and buttons all down the front. It came in at the waist to show how thin she was.

The dance was held in the mess. We could hear the music before we even got there. It was Glen Miller's 'Take the "A" Train'. We stood outside the door, checking our appearance in our compact mirrors. Then we put on our dance shoes and made our grand entrance.

Already the place was crowded with airmen and local girls, mostly from Harkside. The dance floor was busy and a knot of people stood laughing and drinking by the bar. Others sat at the rickety tables smoking and chatting.

'Take your coats, ladies?'

'Why, thank you,' said Gloria.

It was Gloria who had turned the heads, of course.

We handed our coats to the young airman, who was tall, slim and dark in complexion. He spoke with a lazy drawl. He had brown eyes, short black hair and the whitest teeth I had ever seen.

'Over here.' He led us to the far wall, beside the bar, where everyone's coats hung. 'They'll be safe here. And now, ma'am,' he said, turning straight away to Gloria, 'if I may have the pleasure of the first dance?'

Gloria inclined her head slightly, passed her handbag to me, and went off. It didn't take long before someone snapped up Cynthia, too, and I was holding three handbags. But a rather handsome young navigator called Bernard, from Hackensack, New Jersey, asked me to dance before his friend asked Alice. I passed the three handbags to her and left her standing there gawping.

After 'Kalamazoo', 'Stardust' and 'April in Paris', we gathered at the bar and the tall airman bought us all bourbon. His name was Billy Joe Farrell. He hailed from Tennessee and worked on the ground crew. He introduced us to his friend, Edgar Konig, who everyone called PX because on American bases PX meant the quartermaster's stores, which he ran. PX was a gangly young Iowan with a baby face and his fair hair shaved almost to his skull. He was tall, with Nordic cheekbones, pouting lips and the longest eyelashes over his cornflower-blue eyes. He was also very shy. He was the sort of person who never really gets noticed, and I think the reason he was so generous to us all was simply that it made him feel needed.

When I look back on that evening now, it seemed a whirl of dancing, talking and drinking, and it finished before it really began.

As the four of us walked tipsily back through the woods, arms linked with our gallant escorts, we sang 'Shenandoah' and after good-night kisses agreed to meet them in Harkside the next week.

IT WAS THE FIRST TIME Banks had been to the Queen's Arms for lunch in some months. Cyril, the landlord, welcomed him back like a long-lost friend, and Glenys, Cyril's wife, gave him her usual shy smile. He bought a pint and ordered a Yorkshire pudding filled with roast beef and onion gravy. The pub was busy, but he found a small, copper-topped table in a far corner.

He had brought with him a folder DS Hatchley had just dropped on his desk: information gleaned from the central registry of births, marriages and deaths. Already that morning he had phoned army records and asked about Matthew Shackleton's service history. They said they would call him back.

Hatchley's notes confirmed that Gloria was born on September 17, 1921. The official record listed Mile End as her place of birth.

Next, Hatchley had pulled death certificates for Gloria's parents, dated September 15, 1940, listing the same Mile End address and 'injuries sustained during bombing' as the cause of death.

Hatchley had been unable to find a death certificate for Gloria Kathleen Shackleton, but he did find one for Matthew, and the information on it caused Banks almost to choke on his beer.

Matthew Shackleton died on March 15, 1950, by his own hand. Cause of death was given as a 'self-inflicted gunshot wound'. At the time, he was thirty-one years of age, of no occupation, living at an address in Bramley, Leeds. The informant of his death was listed as Gwynneth Vivian Shackleton, of the same address.

He thought for a moment. Matthew Shackleton was supposed to have died in Burma, but obviously he hadn't. The three survivors of the old Hobb's End days that Banks and Annie had talked to had not mentioned Matthew Shackleton's returning, so he must have come back after they had left.

Which made him a definite suspect in his wife's murder.

And why had he killed himself?

Banks carried on reading. A marriage certificate existed for

Gwynneth Vivian Shackleton and Ronald Maurice Bingham. They were married on August 21, 1954. Ronald died of liver cancer at home on July 18, 1967. There was no death certificate for Gwynneth.

Hatchley had also discovered a child born to Gloria Kathleen Stringer at her parents' home address in Mile End, London, on November 5, 1937, shortly after her sixteenth birthday. The boy was christened Francis Paul Henderson, taking his father's surname. George Henderson was listed as 'dock worker'. There was no trace of a marriage certificate.

So Gloria had given birth over three years before she first appeared in Hobb's End. Had she turned the boy's care over to George Henderson? Was this the man who had turned up with the boy at Bridge Cottage during the war?

Glenys brought over Banks's huge stuffed Yorkshire pudding. He tucked into it, washing each mouthful down with a sip of beer.

According to Hatchley's final search, George Henderson had died of a heart attack just five months ago. There was no death or marriage certificate for his son Francis. Why hadn't Gwynneth Shackleton and Francis Henderson come forward? One possibility was that neither of them knew what was going on, which was too much of a coincidence for Banks to swallow. Maybe they had something to hide. But everything that had happened in Hobb's End had occurred before Francis turned eight, so he was hardly a suspect. Nonetheless, his DNA could help determine whether the skeleton really was Gloria Shackleton's.

Banks sighed, put the files back in his briefcase and walked through the crowds across Market Street. He found a message waiting at the front desk from army personnel, informing him that Matthew Shackleton had been listed as 'Missing presumed dead' in 1943, and that was all they had on him. Curiouser and curiouser. Back in his office, Banks picked up the phone and called Detective Inspector Ken Blackstone at Millgarth Station, in Leeds.

'Alan,' said Blackstone. 'Long time no see.'

There was a coolness and distance in his voice. They hadn't been in touch often over the past year or so, and Banks realised he had probably alienated Ken along with just about everyone else who had tried to be his friend during the dark days. 'You know how it is,' he said.

'Sure. What can I do for you? Don't tell me this is just a social call.'

'Not exactly.'

'I thought not.' Blackstone's tone softened a little. 'Any new developments between you and Sandra?'

'Nothing. Except I've heard she's seeing someone.'

'I'm sorry, Alan.'

'These things happen.'

'Tell me about it. I've been there. Want to get rat-arsed and talk about it some time?'

Banks laughed. 'It'll be a pleasure. By the way, have you ever heard anything on the grapevine about a DS called Annie Cabbot?'

'Can't say as I have. But then I've not exactly been around the grapevine much recently . . . So, then, what can I do for you?'

'Well, I'm looking for the details of a suicide. Leeds. Bramley. Gunshot wound. Name's Matthew Shackleton. Died on the 15th of March, 1950.'

'It could take a while.'

'You mean you're talking minutes instead of seconds?'

Blackstone laughed. 'Hours, more like. I'll get DC Collins to make some phone calls. I'll call you back later.'

'Thanks, Ken,' he said. 'Appreciate it.'

'You'd better. And, Alan . . . Don't be a stranger.'

'I know, I know. Curry and piss-up and talk about girls. Soon as you get the info.'

BILLY JOE AND GLORIA soon became a couple. Billy Joe was seen going alone to Bridge Cottage, and that got the village tongues wagging. Especially when PX was seen going there the next day. He, too, seemed to have taken a shy sort of shine to Gloria, happy to get for her whatever her heart desired. I suggested Gloria tell them to use the back door, where they couldn't be seen, but she just laughed.

Gloria told me she wanted sex and Billy Joe was good at it. I still didn't understand what *it* was all about.

Gloria also needed her Luckies, nylons, lipstick, rouge and

whisky. And PX, of course, would get her all these things at the flutter of an eyelash. Whether she ever granted him any favours in exchange, I can't say for certain, but I doubt it. I couldn't imagine PX actually being *with* a woman in that way. He seemed too shy.

Billy Joe was essentially an aeroplane mechanic, but he could fix anything on wheels. When our Morris van gave up the ghost, Billy Joe came down with PX and a couple of others, fixed it in a jiffy, then the whole gang of us collected Gloria and went to the Shoulder of Mutton for a drink. A curious incident occurred that night.

They were the only Americans in the pub and we were the only women. In addition to getting us plenty of suspicious glances, this also drew a few loud and pointed comments.

'Think about it, Bert,' said one local as we bought our drinks. 'Our lads are over there fighting the Nazis, and them damn Yanks are over here sniffing around our women like tomcats on heat.'

We ignored them and took a table in a quiet corner.

The next time we were ready for drinks, Billy Joe went to the bar. He was drinking pints of watery beer, and I had told him to hold on to his glass because there was a shortage. As he was on his way back, one of the local strapping farm lads who hadn't been called up—something to do with an allergy—called out after him: 'Hey, Yank. Tha's ta'en me glass.'

Billy Joe tried to ignore him, but the man, Seth his name was, lumbered over from the bar and stood right behind Billy Joe. The place went quiet.

'I said that's *my* glass tha's got tha beer in, Yank.'

Billy Joe put the tray down on the table and shrugged. 'Same one ah've had all evening, sir,' he said in that lazy Southern drawl.

'"Same one ah've had all evening, sir."' Seth tried to mock him, but it didn't come out right. 'Well it's mine.'

Billy Joe picked up his glass of beer, turned to face Seth slowly and shook his head. 'Ah don't think so, sir.'

'Well, I bloody do. Gimme it back, Yank.'

Billy Joe nodded in that slow way of his, then he poured the beer all over Seth's feet and held out the glass to him. 'You can take the glass,' he said. 'But the beer was mine. Ah paid for it. And, by the way, sir, ah am not a Yankee.'

Even Seth's friends had started to laugh by now. It was that sort of

fulcrum moment, when so much hangs in the balance.

Seth made the wrong move. He stepped back and raised his fist. Billy Joe's speed amazed me. Before anyone knew what had happened, there was the sound of breaking glass and Seth was screaming, hands over his face, blood gushing out between his fingers.

'Ah am not a Yankee, sir,' Billy Joe repeated, then turned his back and sat down. The mood had soured, nobody wanted anything more to drink, and we all left shortly afterwards.

VIVIAN ELMSLEY GOT UP at about one o'clock, turned on the bedside light and took a sleeping pill. She didn't like the way they made her feel woolly-minded the next morning, but lying tossing and turning all night was exhausting.

Slowly, the chemical insinuated its way into her system. She felt sluggish, her blood heavy as lead. She hovered on the threshold between sleep and waking, where thoughts take on the aspect of dreams.

She pictured Gloria's tilted head as she had appeared on the TV screen in the detail from Stanhope's painting, then Gloria covered in blood that oozed from cuts deep into the gristle of her flesh.

Vivian tried to stop it but she felt as if she were being held down by an anchor hooked deep into the horror. She struggled to wake and, as she did, the telephone rang. She shot up, gasping for air as if she had been drowning.

Without thinking, she picked up the receiver. A lifeline.

The monotone voice said, 'Gwen. Gwen Shackleton.'

'Go away,' she mumbled, her tongue thick and furred.

The voice laughed. 'Soon, Gwen,' the man said. 'Soon.'

BANKS AND ANNIE drove out to the estate from Millgarth police headquarters. Banks parked near Bramley Town End, and he and Annie strolled towards the street where Gwen and Matthew Shackleton had lived. Both were dressed casually; neither looked like a police officer. Sometimes, feelings against all forms of authority ran high on these estates.

'How are we going to approach this?' Annie asked.

'We'll play it by ear.'

It was another hot day; people sat out on their doorsteps or had dragged striped deck chairs onto postage-stamp lawns, where the grass was parched pale brown. Banks couldn't help but be aware of the suspicious eyes following their progress.

The address turned out to be on one of the narrower side streets. Most of the doors had scratched and weathered paintwork, and the whole street looked run-down. All the windows of the old Shackleton house were open and loud music blasted from inside.

Banks knocked on the door. A dog growled inside the house. Finally, the door jerked open and a young skinhead in a red T-shirt and torn jeans stuck his head out, holding a barking Rottweiler by its studded collar. Banks stepped back a couple of paces.

'Who the fuck are you? What do you want?' the skinhead asked. He couldn't have been older than eighteen or nineteen.

'Your mum and dad in?' Banks asked.

He laughed. 'I should think so. They never go anywhere. Trouble is, you'll have a bloody long journey. They live in Nottingham.'

'So *you* live here?'

'Course I fucking do.' The dog was still straining at its collar, drool dripping from its jowls, but it had turned quieter now.

'I'd like some information,' said Banks. 'Can we come in?'

'You must be joking, mate. One step over this threshold and Gazza here'll have you singing soprano in the church choir.'

Banks could believe it. 'Fine,' he said. 'Then maybe you can tell us what we want to know out here? It's the house I'm interested in.'

'Who is it, Kev?' came a woman's voice from inside.

Kev turned round and yelled back, 'Mind yer own business, yer stupid bitch!'

Banks sensed Annie stiffen beside him. He touched her forearm gently.

'How long have you lived here?' Banks asked.

'Two years. What's it to you?'

'I'm interested in something that happened here fifty years ago. Do you know who lived here before you?'

'Haven't a clue, mate. But you can ask the wrinklies over the road. They've been here since the ice age.' He pointed to the middle terraced house directly opposite.

'Thanks,' he said. Annie followed him across the street.

After Banks and Annie had held their warrant cards up to the letterbox for inspection, the deadlock and chain came off and a hunched man, probably somewhere in his early seventies, opened the door. He had a hollow chest, deep-set eyes, a thin, lined face and sparse, black-and-grey hair larded back with lashings of Brylcreem.

He led them into the house. The windows were all shut tight and the living room had the atmosphere of a hot and stuffy funeral parlour; it smelt of cigarette smoke.

'What's it all about, then?' The old man flopped down on a sagging brown corduroy settee.

'The past,' said Banks.

A woman walked through from the kitchen. About the same age as the man, she seemed a little better preserved. She certainly had a bit more flesh on her bones.

The old man reached for his cigarettes and lighter and he coughed when he lit up. What the future holds in store for us smokers if we don't stop, Banks thought glumly.

'Police, Elsie,' the man said. 'They say it's about the past.'

'Aye, well, there's plenty of that about for everyone,' she said. 'Like a cuppa?'

'Please,' said Banks. Annie nodded.

'Sit yerselves down then. I'm Mrs Patterson, by the way. You can call me Elsie. And this is my Stanley.'

Stanley leaned forward and offered his hand. 'Call me Stan,' he said, with a wink. Elsie went to make the tea.

'How long have you lived here?' Banks asked.

'For ever. Or so it seems,' Stan said. 'It weren't really such a bad place when we first moved in.'

Elsie soon came back with the tea.

'Stan was just telling me you've lived here a long time,' Banks said to her.

'Since we got married,' she said. 'This was our first home together.' She poured the tea into heavy white mugs and sat down beside her husband.

'And our last, way things turned out,' Stan said.

'Well, whose fault were that? You knew I wanted to move to that new Raynville Estate when they built it, didn't you?'

'Aye,' said Stan. 'And where is it now? They've had to knock the bloody place down now, things got so bad.'

'What year was it?' Banks butted in. 'When you came?'

'In 1949,' Elsie said. 'October 1949. I remember because I were three months gone with Derek at the time.'

'Do you remember anything about your neighbours across the street?' Annie asked.

Elsie spoke first. 'Weren't that those, you know, those . . . what's-their-names, Stanley? A bit stuck up. There were some trouble. That tall skinny young fellow, never said a word to anyone. Shot himself. What were his name?'

'Matthew Shackleton.'

'That's right. We had police all over the place.'

'Did you know the Shackletons?' Banks asked.

'Not really,' Elsie said. 'I tried to be friendly, you know, like you do. The time or two I did talk to her, she didn't say owt about where they came from, except to mention that things had been different back in the village, like. Well, la-di-da, I thought.'

Well, Banks thought, from Hobb's End to this Leeds council estate would have been quite a frightening journey into purgatory for Gwen and Matthew, unless they were in a purgatory of their own making already.

'How many of them lived there?'

'Just the two,' Elsie said. 'I remember her saying her mother used to live with them, but she died a year or so before.'

'Aye,' Stan chipped in. 'I remember them now. Just the two of them. Him and his wife. Tall, gangly lass, herself.'

'Nay,' said Elsie, 'she were never his wife. They didn't act like man and wife.'

'Don't be so bloody daft, woman,' Stan said. Then he looked at Banks. 'She were his wife. Take it from me.'

'What was her name?' Banks asked.

'Blodwyn,' said Stan. 'Summat Welsh, anyroad.'

'No, it weren't. Gwynneth, that were it.'

'What did she look like?'

'Ordinary, really, apart from them beautiful eyes of hers,' said Elsie. 'Like Stanley said, she were a bit taller than your average lass. She had a hard-done-by look about her. Tired, like.'

'Must've been from looking after her husband. He were an invalid. Battle fatigue. War wound.'

'What happened after the suicide?' Banks asked.

'She went away,' Elsie said.

'Do you know where?'

'No. She never even said goodbye. One day she were there, the next she were gone. I'll tell you what, though.' A wicked smile twisted her features. 'I know who that Gwynneth Shackleton is. That's not her name now, of course. Done right well for herself, she has. I've seen her on telly, seen her picture in *Woman's Own*.'

'Yer barmy, woman,' Stan piped up.

'I'm telling you, Stanley: it's her. Those eyes. The height. The voice. I don't forget things like that.'

Banks was trying hard to remain patient and beginning to think he was fighting a losing battle. 'Mrs Patterson. Elsie,' he said finally. 'Could you tell me *who* you think Gwen Shackleton is?'

'That woman writes those detective books. Always on telly. With that good-looking what's-'is-name playing the inspector.'

'She's thinking of that Vivian Elmsley woman,' sighed Stan.

'You don't agree?' Annie asked.

'Nay, I don't know, lass. I'm not good at faces, not the way our Elsie is. There *is* a resemblance, but . . .' He shook his head. 'It's so long ago.'

'Was Gwen in the house at the time of the suicide?' Banks asked.

Elsie paused. 'That's what they asked us back then,' she said. 'I don't know. I *thought* I saw her get back from the shops *before* I heard the bang.' She frowned. 'But I could have been wrong.'

'Did you tell the police this?'

'Yes. But nowt came out of it.'

Now Banks definitely wanted to have a look at the Matthew Shackleton file.

'Well, we might as well be off,' he said to Annie, then turned to Stan and Elsie. 'Thanks very much. You've been a great help.'

'Tell me summat,' said Stan. 'This Gwen, were she his wife?'

'His sister. We think.'

Elsie nudged her husband hard in the ribs. He started coughing. 'See, Stanley. I told yer so, yer great lummox.'

Banks and Annie walked gratefully out into the fresh air.

'What do you think about this Vivian Elmsley business?' Annie asked.

'I'm surprised that neither Betty nor Alice mentioned it.'

'Maybe they didn't know? Alice seems to have very poor eyesight, and Betty Goodall pays little attention to current affairs.'

'True,' said Banks. 'It's definitely worth looking into.'

'So,' said Annie back in the car. 'What next?'

'The local nick. I want to see Matthew Shackleton's file. Then back to Millgarth.'

'Have we time for a drink and a bite to eat later?'

'Sorry. I've got a date.'

She thumped him playfully. 'Seriously?'

'Seriously. With a detective inspector. A *male* detective inspector called Ken Blackstone.'

Banks explained his tenuous friendship with Ken and how he was in the mood for building bridges. He realised that he had been neglecting his friends for too long.

'I see,' Annie said. 'A boys' night out, then?' If she was disappointed, she didn't show it.

BILLY JOE WAS CONFINED to base for a few weeks. They said his punishment would have been far more severe had not all the witnesses attested that he didn't start the fight. Gloria never said as much, but I think the incident put her off Billy Joe. Violence upset her.

It was while Billy Joe was confined to base that we first met Brad and Charlie.

We were walking out of the Lyceum. It was a miserable February night in 1944, not snowing, but freezing cold. We had been to see Bette Davis and Paul Henreid in *Now, Voyager*, and we were both humming the theme song as we put our coats back on in the foyer.

A young man in a fleece-lined leather jacket walked over, put two cigarettes in his mouth, lit them, then handed one to Gloria, as they had done in the film. We doubled over laughing.

'Brad,' said the young man. 'Brad Szikorski. And this is my pal Charlie Markleson.'

Gloria did a little mock curtsy. 'Charmed to meet you, I'm sure.'

'We're with the 448th, over at Rowan Woods. I don't mean to be forward,' said Brad, 'but would you ladies care to honour us by joining us for a drink?'

We exchanged glances. I could tell Gloria wanted to go. Brad was tall and handsome, with a twinkle in his eye and a little Clark Gable moustache. I looked at Charlie, who was probably destined to be my companion for the evening. He had intelligent eyes and a rather pale, thin face. His nose was too big, and it had a bump in the middle, but then mine was nothing to write home about, either. He also seemed reserved and serious. All in all, he'd do.

We walked to the Black Swan. Brad went to the bar and came back bearing a tray of drinks. We toasted one another and drank.

'What do you do?' Gloria asked.

'I'm a pilot,' said Brad, 'and Charlie here's my navigator.'

'A pilot! How exciting. Where are you from?'

'California.'

Gloria clapped her hands together. 'Hollywood!'

'Well, not exactly. A little place called Pasadena.'

'But you must know Hollywood?'

Brad smiled, revealing straight white teeth. 'As a matter of fact, yeah, I do,' he said. 'I did a little stunt flying there in the movies before I came over here.'

'You mean you've actually been in pictures?'

'Well, yeah, I guess so.' He named a couple of titles we hadn't heard of. 'That's what I want to do when all this is over,' he went on. 'Get in the movie business, have a shot at being a stunt man.'

As Gloria and Brad chatted away excitedly about films and Hollywood, Charlie and I started our own hesitant conversation.

He asked me what I did, nodding his head every now and then as I told him. Then he told me that he had completed his English degree just before the war, and wanted to go to Harvard to study law. The more we talked, the more we found we had in common—Jane Austen and Thomas Hardy, for example, and the poetry of T. S. Eliot. And Robert Frost and Edward Thomas. He hadn't heard of many of our younger poets, so I offered to lend him some issues of Penguin New Writing.

'Have you got a husband?' I overheard Brad ask Gloria. 'I mean, I don't mean to . . . You know . . .'

'It's all right. I did have. But he's dead. Killed in Burma. At least I hope to God he was.'

I turned from Charlie. There was still a lingering hope, at least in my mind, and I thought that was a terrible thing to say. I told her so.

She turned on me, eyes flashing. 'You must know what they're saying about the way the Japanese treat their prisoners?'

I had to admit that I had read one or two rather grim stories alleging that torture and decapitation were favourite pastimes in the Japanese POW camps. If the stories were true, then I should probably agree with Gloria and hope Matthew was dead.

'I've got friends fighting in the Pacific,' said Charlie. 'I hear it's pretty rough out there.'

'Well, he's dead, anyway,' said Gloria. 'Look, this is too depressing. Can we have another round of drinkies, please?'

Brad and Charlie drove us home in their Jeep. Charlie seemed a little embarrassed when Brad and Gloria started kissing passionately by the fairy bridge, but he managed to pluck up the courage to put his arm round me. We kissed dutifully and arranged to meet again soon. Brad told Charlie to drive on, that he'd walk back to the base alone later, and he followed Gloria into Bridge Cottage.

THE INDIAN RESTAURANT Ken Blackstone had chosen was a hole-in-the-wall on Burley Road. Sitar music droned from speakers high on the walls, and the aromas of cumin and coriander filled the air.

'Did you find what you were looking for in those incident reports?' Blackstone asked as they shared poppadoms, samosas and pakoras.

'I wasn't after anything in particular,' Banks said. 'Elsie Patterson was unsure as to whether she saw Gwen Shackleton enter the house before or after she heard the shot. And she was the only witness. Nobody else saw Gwen or Matthew that day.'

'What did Gwen Shackleton say in her statement?'

'She just said she found Matthew dead in the armchair when she got home from shopping.'

'Was there any real doubt? Was she ever a suspect?'

'I didn't get that impression. Matthew Shackleton had had a history of mental illness since the war. He was also an alcoholic. According to the report, he had tried to kill himself once before, head in the gas oven that time. A neighbour smelt gas and saved him.'

'It was just a matter of time?'

'Seems that way. Though I suppose there's always the possibility that he was helped on his way, that he had become an intolerable burden to his sister. Remember, Gwen had been taking care of both her mother *and* her brother. It's not much of a life for a young woman, is it? But we'd never prove it.'

'Not unless Gwen Shackleton confessed.'

Their main courses arrived: rogan josh and king prawns, with aloo gobi, pilau rice, lime chutney and chapattis.

'What about forensics?' Blackstone asked.

'Single shot in the mouth. No evidence of a struggle. Empty whisky bottle by the chair. The angle of the wound was also consistent with the suicide theory.'

'Note?'

'Yes. The genuine article, according to forensics.'

'So what's bothering you?'

Banks ate some curry and washed it down with lager before answering. 'Nothing, really. I'm not very interested in whether Gwen Shackleton helped her brother commit suicide or not. But I *would* like to know if he murdered Gloria Shackleton.'

'Perhaps he couldn't live with the guilt?'

'It's the most likely explanation. The only person who can tell us is Gwen Shackleton.'

'What happened to her? Is she still alive?'

'That's another interesting thing. Elsie Patterson swears she's Vivian Elmsley.'

Blackstone whistled. 'The writer?'

'That's the one. We'll have to talk to her. She certainly hasn't been in touch with us. But it's hard to imagine that many people don't know the story.'

'Which may mean that, if it is her, she has a reason for not wanting to be found?'

'Exactly. A guilty secret.'

Blackstone ordered a couple more pints of lager. Then he asked, 'This DS, Annie Cabbot. Good-looking woman?'

'I suppose so.'

'You involved with her?'

Banks paused. Why lie? Ken was a mate. He nodded briefly.

'Is it serious?'

'For crying out loud, Ken, I've only known her a week.'

Blackstone held his hand up. 'OK, OK. Just be careful, that's all. You're still vulnerable. When someone goes through what you're going through, he either ends up angry for a long time or he misses what he had. Or both. If he's angry at women he probably just shags them and leaves them. But if he misses the relationship, then he looks for another one to replace it, and his judgment isn't necessarily in the best of nick. If he's both, then he gets into another relationship and screws it up royally all round and wonders why everyone ends up in tears.'

Banks stood up. 'Well, thanks for the amateur psychology, Ken, but if I'd wanted Claire fucking Rayner—'

Blackstone grabbed on to Banks's sleeve. 'Alan. Sit down. Please. I'm not suggesting you do anything except be aware of the pitfalls. That's all the wisdom I have to offer.' He smiled. 'You've always struck me as a bit of a romantic underneath it all.'

Banks hesitated, still half ready to leave and half ready to punch Blackstone. 'What do you mean?'

'The kind of detective who cares just a bit too much about every victim. The kind of bloke who falls a little bit in love with every woman he sleeps with.'

Banks reached for a cigarette. He felt uncomfortable, as if he were in the dentist's chair and Blackstone were probing a particularly sensitive nerve.

'Alan,' Blackstone went on, 'ten months ago you thought you had a stable marriage. Then, all of a sudden, you find you've got nothing of the kind. The emotional fallout from that sort of upset doesn't go away overnight, mate, I can tell you. Enjoy yourself. Just don't make it more than it is. You're not ready to deal with that yet. Don't confuse sex and love.' He slapped the table. 'Shit, now I *am* starting to sound like Claire Rayner. Ignore me.'

Banks finished his pint. 'Look, I take your point, Ken, but to be honest, it's the first time I've felt comfortable with a woman since Sandra left—the first time I've really felt free enough to jump into something and say damn the consequences.'

Blackstone laughed and shook his head slowly. 'Sounds like you've got it bad.' He looked at his watch. 'What say we hit the fleshpots of Leeds and get irredeemably pissed?'

Banks smiled. 'Most sensible thing you've said all night.'

WINTER FINALLY GAVE WAY to a slow spring, with its snowdrops in Rowan Woods, then the bluebells, crocuses and daffodils. Brad and Charlie became our regular 'beaux' and we saw far less of Billy Joe, who became very sulky. I was worried that Billy Joe would start a fight, given his violent streak, but he soon found another girl and started talking to us again when we met at dances and in pubs. He pestered Gloria on occasion to go back with him, but she was able to keep him at bay, even when she'd been drinking. PX, of course, remained absolutely essential, so we still cultivated him.

I won't say that my affair with Charlie was a grand passion, but we became less awkward with the physical side of things, and he did become the first man I ever slept with. He was gentle, patient and sensitive, and I came to look forward to those times we spent in bed together at Bridge Cottage, courtesy of Gloria. Our relationship remained more of an intellectual one; we passed books back and forth with abandon. Charlie wasn't dull and dry, though; he loved to dance and was a great Humphrey Bogart fan. He took me to see *Casablanca* and *The Maltese Falcon.*

When Michael Stanhope had an exhibition in Leeds, Charlie and I made a weekend of it and went to stay at the Metropole Hotel. Charlie, who knew a lot more about painting than I did, praised the exhibition to the skies. Even Gloria went to see Mr Stanhope at his studio that summer and autumn more often than she had before.

I tried not to dwell on the dangers inherent in Charlie's job and, for his part, he never seemed to want to talk about them. The war receded into the distance during those hours we spent together reading or making love.

In May, when it was warmer, we would often sit on the banks of Harksmere and read Coleridge and Wordsworth out loud to one another. We had picnics of Spam and potted-shrimp sandwiches.

Mother liked Charlie, I could tell, though she didn't say much. She never did. Matthew's disappearance had taken most of the wind out of her sails.

After the excitement of the Normandy landing, things slowly began to improve. The blackout was replaced by the 'dim-out' in September. If by autumn, then, we were feeling flush with the possibility of victory, we had little idea of the grim winter to come.

BY TEN O'CLOCK that night Annie was feeling so restless that even a large glass of wine didn't help settle her down.

She felt disappointed that Banks would rather go drinking with someone else than be with her. True, it was she who had suggested they limit their time together to weekends, but it was also she who had broken the rule the other night. Why couldn't he do the same?

But at least she hadn't wasted *her* time that evening. The long trail that had started on Wednesday, over the telephone, was beginning to bear fruit.

At first, she had come to the conclusion that it was easier finding a fully dressed woman in the *Sunday Sport* than getting information out of the American Embassy. She was shunted from one minion to another for the best part of an hour. By the end of the day, she managed to discover that the personnel at Rowan Woods in late 1943 would have been members of the United States Eighth Air Force, and one of the more helpful employees suggested that she try contacting the National Personnel Records Center in St Louis, Missouri. She checked the time difference and after a little more shunting around was put through to a woman called Mattie, who just 'adored' her accent. Mattie told her she would see what she could do. When Annie mentioned the initials 'PX', Mattie laughed and said that was the man who looked after the store. She also warned Annie that some of their records had been burnt in a fire a few years ago, but if she still had Rowan Woods, she'd fax it. Annie thanked her profusely and felt absurdly pleased with herself.

But it didn't last.

Sometimes when she felt irritable and restless like this, she would go for a drive, and that was exactly what she did now. Without making a conscious decision, she took the road west out of Harkside, and when she reached the turnoff for Thornfield Reservoir, she turned right.

By then she had realised that Banks wasn't the problem; *she* was. She was pissed off at herself for letting him get to her. She was behaving like some sort of silly, love-struck schoolgirl. Vulnerable. Hurt. Let's face it, Annie, she told herself, life has been pretty simple for some time now. No real highs; no real lows. She had been protecting her emotions from the harsh world 'out there'. Sometimes when you open yourself up to that life again, it can be painful. Your emotions are tender and raw, more than usually sensitive to little hurts and humiliations. So that was what was happening.

She pulled into the car park and got out. Silence. A misshapen harvest moon hung low in the western sky.

She took the narrow footpath towards Hobb's End. Hardly any moonlight penetrated the tree cover, but here and there she caught a slat or two of reddish-silver light between branches. She could smell the loamy, earthy smell of trees and shrubs.

Annie reached the slope and paused, looking down on the ruins of Hobb's End. Then she skipped down the slope and walked towards the fairy bridge. From there, she looked along the river and saw the blood-red moonlight reflected in the few little puddles of water that remained on its muddy bed. She walked on past the outbuilding where Gloria's skeleton had been found, and the ruins of Bridge Cottage next to it, and headed down what was once the High Street.

As she went, Annie tried to visualise the scene from Michael Stanhope's painting: children laughing and splashing in the river shallows; knots of local women gossiping outside a shop; the butcher's boy riding like the wind; the tall young woman arranging newspapers in a rack. *Gwynneth Shackleton*. That was who it was. Why hadn't she realised it before?

She looked at the ruins to her right and saw where once there was a detached cottage with a little garden, a row of terraced houses opening directly onto the pavement. Here was the Shackletons' newsagent's shop, here the butcher's, and a little farther down stood the Shoulder of Mutton. So real did it all seem that she began to fancy she could even hear long-silent voices.

As she stood at the western end of the village and breathed in the air deeply, she realised how much she wanted to know what had happened here, every bit as much as Banks did. She identified with Gloria. This was a woman who had struggled and dared to be a little different in a time that didn't tolerate such behaviour. She had lost her parents, then had come to a remote place and fallen in love.

Suddenly, Annie noticed a movement and saw a figure scuttle across the fairy bridge. Her blood froze.

Finding her voice, she called out. No answer came. The figure disappeared into the woods. Annie set off in pursuit.

Just when she had got back up the slope, and was heading for the woods, she heard a car start ahead of her. There were two small car parks, separated by a high hedge, and whoever this was must have been parked in the other one, or Annie would have seen the car earlier. She put on an extra burst of speed but could only get to the road in time to see the taillights disappearing.

Chapter Six

'He asked me to marry him,' Gloria repeated.

'I still don't believe you,' I said.

It was early in the new year, 1945, and I had dropped by Bridge Cottage to see how Gloria was coping: she had had a terrible cold over Christmas—had even missed Alice Poole's farewell party. Though she was pale, she seemed to be on the mend.

'Well, you can ask him yourself. It's true. You should have seen my nose when he asked me. It was red-raw.'

I laughed. It was good to laugh at something. Christmas that year had been a miserable affair because the advance that had seemed to be going so well earlier had bogged down in the Ardennes.

'What did you say?' I asked.

'I told him I'd think about it, but he'd have to wait until we could find out for certain about Matt.'

'Do you love him?'

'In a way. Not . . . Oh, I mean I don't really think I could ever love anyone like I loved Matt, but Brad and I get on well enough. And he's good to me. When the war's over, he wants to take me back to Hollywood with him.'

'It'll be a new lease of life, I suppose.'

'Yes.'

'And I'll have someone I can visit out there.'

'You will.'

'But? I still sense a "but".'

'Oh, I don't know, Gwen. You know I can't even consider getting married again until the war's over, for a start. But I will think about it. What about Charlie? Has he asked you yet?'

I blushed. 'No,' I said.

'Books, that's all you two ever talk about.'

'It's not.'

She smiled. 'I'm teasing, Gwen. I'm glad you're happy. Honest, I am. There's no hurry, I suppose. But you could do a lot worse. A lawyer! He'll be rich, just you wait and see. You can go to America, too. We can see each other all the time.'

'Gloria, Boston is miles away from Los Angeles.'

'Is it? Well, at least we'll be in the same country.'

And so we chatted on about what the future might offer us. Gloria soon recovered her health, and February brought the prospect of victory closer. I actually began to believe that we were entering the last spring of the war.

Everything changed one grey afternoon in March, when a tall, gaunt stranger walked down the High Street towards me, struggling against the wind.

BANKS REALLY MUST have had a night on the tiles, Annie thought. It was after nine, and he wasn't in his office yet. Was he still in Leeds? Had he and his friend picked up some women?

She fought back the acid-burn of jealousy that curdled in her stomach. Jealousy and suspicion had ruined relationships for her before. Just before Rob got killed she had suspected he was seeing someone else and had consequently treated him badly. She thought she had learned detachment, but perhaps she had only put her insecurity in mothballs. It was a frightening thought.

The fax machine hummed into action. Annie hurried over. It was a personnel breakdown of the 448th Bomber Group based at Rowan Woods between December 19, 1943 and May 17, 1945, when they had left. There were a lot of names.

As she glanced over the list, Annie thought again about the Hobb's End incident last night. It had rattled her more than she realised at first, and she had had a difficult time getting to sleep. *Why* should someone hide from her, and then why take off when she gave chase? There was nothing left at the site; the SOCOs had been over it thoroughly. Perhaps someone might *think* there was something there, though. Whoever it was hadn't been old enough to have murdered Gloria Shackleton over fifty years ago: people in their seventies or eighties don't usually move that fast.

So it remained a mystery. She wanted to talk to Banks about it, but he'd been off getting pissed with his mates. She hoped he had a hangover the size of China.

BANKS GOT BACK to Gratly safe and sane via the slow back roads. He didn't want Annie to see him until he had managed a change of clothes. The ones he was wearing stank of smoke and stale beer.

His head ached, despite the paracetamol he had downed at Ken's flat that morning. When he had woken up and looked around Ken's living room, he had groaned at the detritus of a wild and foolish night: an empty bottle of Glenmorangie on the coffee table, alongside an empty bottle of claret and an overflowing ashtray. Even a fifteen-year-old would have had more sense than to mix lager, wine and whisky that way. All the hangover clichés ran through his mind: *You're getting too old for this sort of thing* and *I'll never touch another drop as long as I live*.

After a shave, a shower and a change of clothes, Banks drove to his office. He hardly had time to turn on his computer when his door opened and in strode Chief Constable Jeremiah 'Jimmy' Riddle himself, making one of his rare forays to Eastvale. Banks muttered a silent curse. Just what he needed.

'Banks, you look bloody awful,' said Riddle. 'What have you been doing, man? Drinking yourself silly?'

'Touch of flu, sir. What can I do for you, sir?'

'Flu, my arse. I hope you're on top of things?'

'Definitely, sir.'

'Good. I want you to bring me up to date on that skeleton case. I've got to go to London today to tape an interview for *Panorama*. They're putting together a special segment on the investigation of old cases, how DNA makes a difference, that sort of thing.' He brushed some imaginary fluff from the front of his uniform. 'And you'd better make it quick. My train leaves in an hour and a half.'

Well, be thankful for small mercies, Banks told himself. He told him what he and Annie had discovered so far.

Riddle ran his hand over his shiny bald scalp and said, 'It's not much to go on, is it? Memory of a couple of old biddies?'

'We're not likely to get much better,' said Banks. 'Too much time's gone by. Anyway, we're still waiting for results of DNA tests from Dr Williams and our forensic odontologist. These things take time.'

'And cost money. Don't think I'm not keeping my eye on the bottom line on this one, Banks.'

'You mentioned DNA, sir,' Banks said. 'You might mention that it would be a great help if Gloria Shackleton's son could get in touch with us. That way we could verify the identity of the remains once and for all.'

Riddle stood up. 'If I've got time, Banks. If I've got time. By the way,' he said. 'DS Cabbot. How's she working out?'

She. So he did know. 'Fine,' said Banks. 'She's a good detective. Wasted in a place like Harkside.'

A malicious smile flitted across Riddle's face. 'Ah, yes. Pity, really. I understand there was some trouble in her previous posting.'

'Trouble, sir?'

'You should know all about that, Banks. Insubordination, failure to respect senior ranks.'

'I respect the rank, sir,' said Banks. 'But not always the person who fills it.'

Riddle stiffened. 'Well, I hope you're enjoying yourself—for your sake, Banks—because this is about as good as it's going to get.'

With that he walked out and slammed the door.

On his way to the coffee machine, Banks asked DS Hatchley to find out what he could about Francis Henderson, Gloria's illegitimate child. It was a loose end that nagged him.

Back at his desk there was a message from a Major Gargrave, in military personnel. Banks phoned him back.

'It's about that query you made the other day,' said Major Gargrave. 'Matthew Shackleton. It's all a bit embarrassing really.'

'He came back, didn't he? We found a death certificate dated 1950. I was going to ask you about it.'

'Yes, well, when my assistant was returning the file, he found some papers wedged down between two folders. It was a filing error.'

'When did he return?' Banks asked.

'March 1945. Place called Hobb's End. Does that make any sense?'

'Yes,' said Banks. 'Go on.'

'Sergeant Shackleton simply discharged himself from a London hospital and went home. The hospital said he'd been liberated from a Japanese POW camp and shipped home in pretty bad shape. No identification.'

'And that's all?'

'Yes. It would seem so. Very odd.'

'OK,' said Banks, 'thanks very much for calling, Major.'

After he hung up, Banks opened the window and let the sunshine in. He thought of lighting a cigarette but his throat and lungs still felt raw. There was something that didn't make sense in what the major had just told him, but he couldn't quite work out what. Too many dead brain cells in the way.

Banks steeled himself and picked up the phone. Annie answered on the third ring.

'You're back, then.' Her tone was icy.

'Yes.'

'Have a good time?'

'Pretty good, thanks. I'd rather forget this morning, though.'

'You probably deserve it.'

'Probably.'

'I've got the info on the Rowan Woods personnel.'

'Wonderful.'

'It's a long list, though. It'll take a bit of whittling down. There was more than one person working in the PX, for a start.'

'Is there anything else?'

Annie told him about what happened at Hobb's End.

'It was probably just a kid.'

'It didn't look like a kid. And it drove away.'

'There's not much we can do about it now, though, is there?'

'I just thought I'd let you know. For the record.'

'We'd better track down Vivian Elmsley,' Banks said.

'I've already done that.'

'Now I'm *really* impressed.'

'So you should be. While you've been recovering from your self-inflicted damage, I've been on the phone.'

Banks sensed that her tone was softening a little. 'And?'

'Well, in her case it was easy. She's in the London telephone directory. I've got her address. What do you want to do about it?'

'We should talk to her as soon as possible. If she really is the one we're looking for, she's holding something back. There was another thing nagging at me and I've just realised what it was.' Banks explained to her about the call from Major Gargrave. 'Why would Matthew have a gun? If he was a released POW, he'd hardly have his service revolver. I should imagine the Japanese confiscated the weapons from the people they captured, wouldn't you?'

'Unless his liberators gave him one?'

'I suppose that's just possible. Especially if they were Americans. Americans feel naked without guns.'

'But you don't think so?'

'I think it's highly unlikely. Why should they? And why would he still have it when he went back to Hobb's End from hospital?'

'If he did have a gun, though, why didn't he use that on Gloria instead of strangling her and stabbing her?'

'*If* it was Matthew who killed her.'

'Have you considered Gwen as a serious suspect?' Annie asked.

'Certainly. According to everything we've heard, she was very close to her brother. If Gloria was hurting him, running around with other men, Gwen might just have fought back on his behalf. At the very least she should be able to tell us more about Matthew's relationship with Gloria after he came back. Fancy a trip to London tomorrow? There's a train leaves York at around a quarter to nine that'll have us to King's Cross by twenty to eleven. Can you manage that?'

'No problem.'

After Annie hung up, Banks tried dialling Brian's Wimbledon number again. Still nothing. He hoped he might be able to see Brian tomorrow, have a talk, get things sorted. He didn't want Brian to keep on thinking he was disappointed in him.

He went back to his desk. For about the third time since the case began, he spread out the objects found with Gloria Shackleton's body. Detective Superintendent Gristhorpe might be able to tell him a bit about the button, he thought. Gristhorpe was a bit of an expert on military history, especially the Second World War.

Banks grabbed his jacket and was just about to leave the office when his phone rang.

'Hello, Alan.' A woman's voice.

'Yes?'

'It's Jenny. Jenny Fuller.'

He hadn't seen Jenny Fuller in almost a year, not since she'd decided to take a leave of absence from York University to teach in California.

'Jenny. It's been a long time. Where are you?'

'Home. Just got back yesterday.'

'A bit early, aren't you?'

'It's a long story.'

'I'm glad you called. I need some professional advice.'

'I might be able to manage that. The reason I'm phoning is, I'm in town and I wondered if you've got time for lunch?'

Banks had intended to drive out to Lyndgarth to see Gristhorpe, who was taking his annual holiday at home, but that could wait until later. 'Queen's Arms, half twelve?'

'Wonderful. I'll see you there.'

Banks smiled as he put down the receiver. His colleagues had expected him to sleep with Jenny Fuller after Sandra left. Perhaps he would have if she had been around. But timing is everything. Jenny was spending most of her time in California these days, and there was a man involved.

Now he and Jenny were having lunch in about an hour's time. Just enough time, in fact, to nip over to Waterstone's for a couple of Vivian Elmsley's novels. Her writing might give him some insight into her character.

For some reason I was standing out in the street to check the window display when I glanced to my left and saw him coming across the fairy bridge. He was wearing a baggy brown suit and carrying no luggage. He was tall but stooped, as if suffering some affliction of the spine, and he walked with a stick. He moved slowly, as if he knew where he was going, but felt no hurry to get there. His frame was thin to the point of emaciation. As he came closer, I realised that he wasn't as old as I had first thought, though his lank, lifeless hair was tinged with grey.

The wind tugged at my clothes and chilled me to the marrow, but something about him compelled me to stand and watch, as if in a trance. When he got within a few feet, I saw his eyes. Deep, hollow, haunted eyes, turned completely inwards.

I don't know when the truth dawned on me; it could have been seconds; it could have been minutes. But I started to shake like a leaf. I ran to him and threw my arms round him but his body felt stiff and unyielding. Tears were pouring down my cheeks.

'Matthew!' I cried. 'Oh my God. Matthew!'

Banks walked into the Queen's Arms a couple of minutes before twelve thirty, carrying two of Vivian Elmsley's paperback mysteries. He bought a pint and sat down at a table.

One was a suspense novel called *Guilty Secrets*—an interesting title from Banks's point of view—which bore review quotes to the effect that it was an 'amazing' and 'disturbing' achievement by one of our best mystery writers. The other was called *The Shadow of Death* and featured her series character, Detective Inspector Niven. The novel was praised for its 'compassionate realism in the portrayal of ordinary people' and its 'believable depictions of policemen's lives and police procedures'. Banks smiled. He'd see about that.

He was on page ten when Jenny dashed in, out of breath, tousled red hair flaming around her face. When she saw him she waved, hurried over and bent to give him a quick peck on the cheek. 'Sorry I'm late. My God, you look awful.'

Banks smiled and raised his glass. 'Hair of the dog.'

Jenny picked up the paperback he had set down on the table. 'I didn't think this sort of thing was up your alley.'

'Work.'

'Aha.' She raised her eyebrows.

Her figure looked as good as ever in tight black jeans and a loose jade silk top, Banks thought.

'So,' he said, when she had settled herself down. 'Can I get you a drink?'

'Campari and soda, please.'

'Food?'

'I've been craving scampi and chips for about a month now.'

'Scampi and chips it is.' Banks made his way to the bar, got them each a drink and ordered the food. He settled for plaice and chips.

He carried the drinks back and found Jenny poring over *The Shadow of Death*. Banks told her briefly about the case so far. By the time he had finished, their food arrived.

'Is it as good as you remembered?' he asked after she had taken a couple of bites.

'Nothing ever is,' Jenny said. He noticed a new sadness and weariness in her eyes. 'It's good, though.'

'What happened over there?'

'What do you mean?' She glanced at him, then looked away quickly. Too quickly. He saw fear in her eyes.

He thought of the first time he had met her in Gristhorpe's office, how he had been struck by her sharp intelligence and her quick sense of humour, as well as her flaming red hair, full lips and green eyes with their attractive laughter lines. His first impression had been that she was a knockout. He felt exactly the same today.

'Come on, Jenny,' he said. 'This sudden return wasn't on the agenda.'

She sighed, looked away, tried to form some words, sighed again. She seemed a lot more twitchy than he remembered, always moving her hands. 'It's all washed up, Alan. The job. Randy. My life.' She cocked her head. 'I never did have much luck with men, did I?'

Banks remembered one or two of Jenny's disasters.

'Just tell me what you want to, at your own pace,' said Banks.

She smiled and patted his arm. 'Thanks. You're sweet.' She snatched a cigarette from his packet and lit up.

'You don't smoke,' Banks said.

'I do now.' Jenny blew out a long plume. 'I've just about had it up to here with those nicotine-nazis out there. And to think California was a real hotbed of protest in the sixties. It's run by fascists now. As I'm sure you've gathered already,' she went on, 'Randy, my paramour, my reason for staying out there, is no longer a part of my life.'

'What happened?'

'Graduate students. Or, to put it more bluntly, blonde twenty-something bimbos with their brains between their legs.'

'I'm sorry, Jenny.'

She waved her hand. 'I should have seen it coming. Anyone else would have. Anyway, soon as I found out about what he was up to, there wasn't much to keep me there.'

'What are you going to do?'

'I'll be going back to my old lecturing job at York. Start next month. If that doesn't work out, I'll go into private practice. I'm quite the expert on deviants and criminal psychology. I've even been on training courses with the FBI profilers.'

'I want to ask your advice on something.'

'Go ahead. I'm finished blubbering and moaning. And I didn't even ask about you. How are *you* doing?'

'I'm doing fine, thanks.'

'Seeing anyone?'

Banks paused a moment. 'Sort of.'

'Serious?'

'What kind of a question is that?'

'So it *is* serious. What was it you wanted to ask me?'

'It's about Matthew Shackleton. Gwen's brother. Apparently he spent a few years in one of the Japanese prison camps. By all accounts, he was pretty disturbed when he came home. Ended up committing suicide. Thing is, all I can come up with in terms of psychiatric diagnoses are such vague terms as "combat fatigue". I was wondering what sort of diagnosis you'd come up with today.'

'That's a good one, Alan. You want me, a *psychologist*, to come up with a *psychiatric* diagnosis of a dead man's mental problems? This had better be between you and me.'

Banks grinned. 'Don't worry, you won't be called upon to testify in court.'

'Well,' Jenny said, 'I'm only guessing, but he was probably suffering from some kind of post-traumatic stress disorder.'

'This condition would have been caused by his experiences in the war and the camp, right?'

'Right. Basically, PTSDs are caused by some event or series of events well beyond the normal range of human experience—things like rape, kidnapping, military combat, earthquakes, fires, car crashes, torture, death camps.'

'I get the picture. What are the symptoms?'

'Recurrent nightmares about the event are common. As is a feeling that the event is recurring—things like flashbacks and hallucinations. Anything that reminds the person of the event is painful, too; also things that were part of it. If a man was kept in a small cage for a long period, for example, then he would be likely to experience suffocating claustrophobia in a lift, for example. Strong feelings of detachment, estrangement and separation come with it. People who suffer from PTSDs often find it difficult to feel or accept love, they become alienated from their families and loved ones. Add to that insomnia, difficulty in concentrating, hypervigilance, panic disorders. Suicide is also not uncommon.'

'Might he be likely to become violent?'

'That's a difficult one. Anyone can become violent given the right stimulus. He would certainly be prone to irritability and outbursts of anger, but I'm not sure they'd necessarily lead to murder.'

'I was thinking he might have killed his wife because he found out she'd been having an affair.'

'I suppose it's possible,' Jenny said.

'But you don't think so?'

'Let me just say I hold reservations. The outbursts of anger in PTSD are usually fairly irrational. By linking them to his wife's behaviour, you're making it all far more logical. Cause and effect. And if he did feel detached and was unable to love, then where does the jealousy come in?'

'So could he or couldn't he?'

'Oh, no, you're not trapping me like that. Of course he *could* have committed murder. People do all the time, often for no reason.'

'Whoever did it probably strangled the woman, then stabbed her about fifteen or sixteen times.'

'Such rage. I don't know, Alan. From what I know of PTSD, I'd say that most of his pain and anger would have been directed inwards, not out at the world. Also, it's often too easy to pick on the mentally disturbed person as the most likely murderer. Most mentally ill people wouldn't harm a fly. Pathetic, perhaps, sometimes scary, but rarely dangerous.'

'Thanks. You've given me a lot to think about.'

They both sat in silence, nursing their drinks. Banks thought about Matthew Shackleton's suffering and his possible alienation from normal human affairs. If you couldn't feel love for someone, why would you feel hate? When Banks first found out about Sandra and Sean, he had hated them both because he still loved Sandra. If he hadn't cared, he wouldn't have felt so passionate.

'I fell apart, you know,' Jenny said suddenly.

'You did what?'

'I had a breakdown. After all that with Randy. I suddenly found myself completely cut off from everyone I'd grown up with, alone in a foreign country. It's one of the scariest feelings I've ever had. I fell to pieces. I even went to see a shrink.'

'Do any good?'

'Some. One of the things I realised was that I wanted to go home. That wasn't part of being ill. I *missed* this place too much. I actually missed winter. It gets you down, all that sun, day in, day out, only the occasional flood, fire or earthquake for variety. Anyway, as soon as I realised what I really wanted to do, I chucked my tranquillisers down the toilet and took the next flight home. Well, almost the next flight. I had a little act of girlish revenge to carry out first.'

'What did you do?'

Jenny flashed him a wicked grin. 'I planted one of those little voice-activated tape recorders in his office and taped one of his trysts. Then I sent the tape to the dean.'

'What happened?'

'I don't know. I left before the shit hit the fan. I should imagine he got suspended. Maybe fired.' She tossed back the rest of her drink and looked at her watch. 'Look, I'm sorry, I'll have to go. It's great seeing you again.'

She picked up her bag and paused. Then she looked Banks in

the eye, and touched his hand softly. 'Why don't you give me a ring? We could . . . you know, have dinner or something together?'

Banks swallowed. 'I will. That would be great.'

She patted his hand, blew him a kiss and then she was gone in a whirl of red, jade and black, leaving a faint trace of Miss Dior behind. Banks looked down at his hand. It still tingled where she had touched him. Now that he had found the courage and desire to start a relationship with Annie, Jenny was a complication he didn't need.

AFTER I HAD RUN and fetched Gloria from the farm, I was finally able to piece together what had happened. Matthew himself would not say a word. He looked at us as if he remembered knowing us once, as if some deep homing instinct had brought him here, but our fussing didn't make much sense to him.

I went down to the telephone and began the long round of calls. The Ministry was about as much help as usual, the Red Cross a little more forthcoming, but it was ultimately a doctor in one of the big London hospitals who told me the most.

Matthew had been found at a Japanese POW camp near Luzon, in the Philippines. All his identification was missing, and all anyone could tell about him, from the scraps of his uniform, was that he was British. He hadn't spoken to any of the other prisoners and none of them had been captured at the same time as he had. Consequently, nobody knew where he had come from.

When I asked the doctor why Matthew wouldn't speak and why he also refused, when offered pen and paper, to write anything down, he paused, then said, slowly, 'I'm sorry to say, but one of the things we found was that his tongue had been cut out.'

I could think of nothing to say. I stood there, head spinning.

'Miss Shackleton? Miss Shackleton? Are you there?'

'I'm sorry . . . Please go on.'

'I'm the one who should be sorry. It must have sounded so abrupt and callous to you. I apologise.'

'That's all right, Doctor . . . So Matthew is incapable of talking?'

'Yes.'

'But he could write if he wanted?'

'There's no reason why not. All I can assume is that he simply

chooses not to communicate. He's probably suffering from some form of combat fatigue.'

'Should we send him back to the hospital?'

'I can't see much point in doing that,' said the doctor. 'Physically, there's nothing more we can do for him. There's some deformity of the spine, probably due to being forced into a cramped environment, like a box or a cage, for long periods of time. A pronounced limp in the left leg, caused by an improperly set fracture. He was also shot in the arm and the abdomen. The wounds are healed now.'

I swallowed. 'And mentally?'

'As I said, we don't really know why he's refusing to communicate. It's a good sign that he came home, though.'

'Is there any treatment? Will he get better?'

'It's impossible to say. There are treatments. Narcosynthesis is the most common. It's a drug-induced re-enactment of the traumatic episodes, used to assist the ego to accept what happened. The problem is, of course, that Matthew can't express himself vocally, and that could mean a severe limitation to the value of narcosynthesis. If you give me your address, I'll put you in touch with a doctor who knows about these things. In the meantime, just take good care of him. I don't think I need to tell you that he has suffered appallingly.'

'No. Thank you, Doctor.' I gave him my address and went back upstairs, where Matthew was sitting staring towards the window. Mother and Gloria seemed at their wits' end.

'I don't think he even knows me.' Gloria said, voice quivering.

I told her what the doctor had said. 'He came back here, didn't he?' I said, to comfort her. 'Home. Don't worry, he'll be fine now he's back with the people who love him.'

Gloria nodded, but she didn't seem convinced. I wasn't either.

AS HE EXPECTED, Banks found Detective Superintendent Gristhorpe out back working on his dry-stone wall. Walling was a hobby the superintendent had taken up years ago. He found it relaxing.

Gristhorpe was wearing a baggy pair of brown corduroy trousers held up by frayed red braces, and a checked shirt. He was holding a triangular lump of limestone in his hand. When Banks approached, he turned. His pockmarked face was redder than usual after the exertion and his unruly mop of hair lay plastered to his skull.

'Alan,' he said. It wasn't a greeting, just a statement.

'Sir.'

'They say a good waller doesn't put a stone aside once he's picked it up,' Gristhorpe said, then looked at the rock in his hand. 'I wish I could figure out where to put this bugger.' He paused, then he tossed the stone back on the pile. 'You'll have a glass of something?'

'Anything cold.'

'Coke, then. I've got some in the fridge. We'll sit out here.' Gristhorpe pointed to two fold-up chairs in the shade by the back wall of the old farmhouse. Banks sat down.

Gristhorpe went inside and returned with two glasses of Coke, and sat down.

'I hear Jimmy Riddle's given you a real case to work on.'

'Sort of. I'm sure he thinks of it as more of a dead end.'

Gristhorpe raised his bushy eyebrows. 'Is it?'

'I don't think so.' Banks told Gristhorpe what he had discovered so far and handed him the button. 'It's impossible to say,' he went on, 'but it *might* have been in the victim's hand. She could have ripped it from her attacker's uniform.'

Gristhorpe examined the button. 'It looks like an American army air force button,' he said. 'It's so corroded it's hard to tell, but that design looks like the American eagle. The button could have come from the collar. Usually it was worn on the right side. Officers wore them left or right with the branch of service below.'

'If she was being strangled,' said Banks, 'then it's quite likely she reached out to try to grab at her attacker's collar.'

Gristhorpe handed the button back. 'It sounds like a reasonable theory to me.'

'There's another thing that puzzles me. Matthew Shackleton committed suicide in 1950. Shot himself. I'm wondering where he got the gun. He was in no state to go out and buy one on the black market.'

'What kind of gun was it?'

'A Colt .45 automatic.'

'Really? That was the gun the American military issued their servicemen. It raises interesting possibilities, doesn't it? American button in the wife's hand. American gun in the husband's mouth.'

Banks nodded. Though what the possibilities were, he hadn't a clue. The two events were separated by five years or more.

'Alan, I might have a bit of good news for you, if you can promise to keep it to yourself.'

'Good news. That makes a change.'

'Between you, me and the stone wall, Jimmy Riddle might not be around much longer. A little bird tells me that the crooked finger of politics beckons. As you know, he can't enter into that as a copper.'

'Politics?'

'Aye. His local Conservative MP is practically gaga. Some high-echelon rumour has it that Riddle has already had several interviews with the selection committee and they're pleased with him.'

Banks began to feel a sort of warm glow deep inside. Maybe his dry season really was coming to an end.

CHARLIE WAS KILLED on March 19 during a big raid over Berlin. Their Flying Fortress got badly shot up by a Messerschmitt. Brad managed to fly the aeroplane back across the Channel and land in an airfield in Sussex. He escaped with cuts and bruises.

When he got back from Sussex, he came over to the shop with a bottle of bourbon and told me the news in person. I could tell he was devastated by what had happened.

Gloria had told Brad she couldn't see him again, that it would only upset her and would do them no good. Brad was angry and upset about her rejection, but there was nothing he could do except come to me and pour his heart out.

We sat in the small room above the shop after Mother had gone to bed and drank bourbon. Neither of us said very much; there was nothing, really, *to* say. Coming right after Matthew's return, this news was almost impossible for me to bear.

Not far down the High Street, Gloria was devoting her time to caring for a man who couldn't speak and wouldn't communicate, with no end in sight. That was what our lives had been reduced to by the war: the essence of misery and hopelessness. I laid my head on Brad's shoulder and cried.

ON THURSDAY EVENING Banks tried Brian's number yet again.

On the fifth ring, someone answered.

'Brian?'

'Andy. Who's calling?'

'His father.'

Pause. 'Just a sec.'

A few moments later, Brian came on the phone. 'Dad?'

'Where've you been? I've been trying to get in touch with you.'

'We were doing some gigs in South Wales. Look, Dad, I told you, we've got gigs coming out of our ears. You weren't interested.'

Banks paused. He didn't want to blow it this time, but he was damned if he was going to grovel to his own son. 'You have to give it a little time to sink in. We were all expecting you to come out with a good degree and start working at a good firm somewhere. It's a shock, that's all. Music's a great hobby but a risky living. Anyway, the main reason I'm calling is that I'll be down in your neck of the woods tomorrow, so I wondered if we could get together. Let me buy you a pint.'

'I don't know, Dad. We're really busy right now.'

'Half an hour?'

Another pause followed. 'Look,' Brian said, 'tomorrow and Saturday we're playing at a pub in Bethnal Green. If you want to come and listen, we can have that pint during the break.'

Banks got the name of the pub and said he'd do his best.

'It's all right,' said Brian. 'I'll understand if something crops up and you can't make it. Wouldn't be the first time. One of the joys of being a copper's son.'

'I'll be there,' said Banks. 'Goodbye.'

It was almost dark. Banks took his whisky and went outside to sit on the wall. A few remaining streaks of crimson and purple shot the sky to the west and the waning moon shone over the valley. The promise of a storm had dissipated and the air was clear and dry again.

Well, Banks thought, at least he had talked to Brian and would get to see him soon.

He heard his phone ring. Quickly, he went back inside.

'Sorry to disturb you at this time of night, sir,' said DS Hatchley, 'but I know you're off to London in the morning.'

'What is it?' Banks looked at his watch. Half past nine. 'It's not like you to be working so late, Jim.'

'I'm not. I mean, I wasn't. I was just over at the Queen's Arms, so I thought I'd pop in the station, like, and see if I'd got any answers to my inquiries.'

'And?'

'Francis Henderson. I've got an address. Dulwich.' Hatchley read the address. 'What's interesting, why it came back so quick, is he's got form.'

Banks's ears pricked up. 'Go on.'

'According to Criminal Intelligence, Francis Henderson started working for one of the East End gangs in the sixties. Not the Krays exactly, but that sort of thing. Mostly he dug up information for them, found people they were after. He developed a drug habit and started dealing to support it in the seventies. They say he's been retired and clean for years now, at least as far as they know.'

'Thanks a lot, Jim. Get yourself home now.'

'Don't worry, I will.'

'And give another push on that nationwide tomorrow if you can find time.'

'Will do. *Bon voyage*.'

Chapter Seven

Annie was waiting at York Station looking very businesslike in a navy mid-length skirt and silver-buttoned blazer over a white blouse. She had tied her hair back. For once, though, Banks didn't feel underdressed. He wore a lightweight cotton summer suit together with a red and grey tie.

'Good Lord,' she said, smiling, 'I feel like we're sneaking away for a dirty weekend.'

Banks laughed. 'If you play your cards right . . .'

The London train pulled out of the station and Banks and Annie chatted for a while, lulled by the rattling and rocking rhythm. Banks ascertained that whatever had been bothering Annie on the phone the day before was no longer a problem. He had been forgiven.

She started reading *The Guardian* and Banks went back to *Guilty Secrets*. In bed the previous evening, he had given up on *The Shadow of Death* when DI Niven arrested his first suspect, saying, 'You have the right to remain silent. If you don't have a lawyer, one will be provided for you.' So much for the realistic depiction of police procedures. Feeling that the author deserved a second chance, he started *Guilty Secrets* and had trouble putting it down. Despite the thinness of the plot, *Guilty Secrets* turned out to be a fascinating exploration of conscience and character. Banks finished the book just before Peterborough. Annie had closed her eyes by then and was either napping or meditating. He gazed out of the window.

King's Cross was the usual madness. Banks and Annie negotiated their way through the crowds and tunnels to the Northern Line and managed to cram into the first Edgware-bound train.

A few minutes later, they came out of Belsize Park tube station, walked up Rosslyn Hill and turned into the side street where Vivian Elmsley lived.

A woman's voice answered over the intercom.

Banks stated his rank and his business. There was a long pause then a resigned voice said, 'You'd better come up.' The lock buzzed.

They walked up three flights of thickly carpeted stairs to the second-floor landing. That this was a well-maintained building was clear from the gleaming woodwork and freshly painted walls. Probably cost an arm and a leg, but then Vivian Elmsley could no doubt afford an arm and a leg.

She was dressed in baggy black exercise trousers and a white sweatshirt. Still, Banks supposed, it didn't matter what you wore if all you had to do was sit around and write all day. She looked tired, bags under her eyes, broken blood vessels crisscrossing the whites. Banks could see what Elsie Patterson meant: there was no mistaking those slanted eyes. She also looked strained and edgy.

'Please, sit down.' She gestured Banks and Annie towards two matching chrome-and-black-leather chairs, then sat down herself. 'How can I help you?'

'First of all,' Banks asked, 'are you Gwynneth Shackleton?'

'I was, though most people called me Gwen. Vivian is my middle name. Elmsley is a pseudonym. Actually, it's my mother's maiden name. It's all perfectly legal.'

'I'm sure it is. You grew up in Hobb's End?'

'Yes.'

'Did you kill Gloria Shackleton?'

Her hand went to her chest. 'Kill Gloria? Me? What a suggestion. I most certainly did not.'

'Could Matthew, your brother, have killed her?'

'No. Matthew loved her. She looked after him.'

'May I ask why you haven't come forward in response to our requests for information?' Banks asked.

Vivian Elmsley paused before answering, as if composing her thoughts carefully. 'Chief Inspector,' she said, 'I admit that I have been following developments both in the newspapers and on television, but I honestly don't believe I can tell you anything of any value. I have also found it all very distressing. That's why I haven't come forward.'

'Oh, come off it,' said Banks. 'Not only did you live in Hobb's End throughout the war and knew the victim well, you were also her sister-in-law. You can't expect me to believe you know nothing at all about what happened toher.'

'I can't honestly say I knew her very well. I wouldn't say we had much in common. I was always a bookish sort of girl, whereas Gloria was the more flamboyant type. As with many extroverts, she was also a secretive person, very difficult to get to know.'

'Did you see a lot of her?'

'Quite a bit. We were in and out of one another's houses. Bridge Cottage wasn't far from the shop.'

'Didn't you ever do things together?'

Vivian shrugged. 'I suppose we did. We went to the pictures, to dances.'

'Dances with American airmen?'

'Sometimes, yes.'

'Was there anyone in particular?'

'I suppose we were quite friendly with several of them.'

'Do you remember their names? What about Brad? Ring a bell?'

'Brad? Yes, I think he was one of them. Brad Szikorski.'

Banks checked the list of Rowan Woods personnel he had brought with him. *Bradford J. Szikorski, Jr.*

'And PX? Billy Joe?'

'Edgar Konig and Billy Joe Farrell.'

They were on the list, too.

'What about Charlie?'

Vivian Elmsley turned pale; a muscle by her jaw began to twitch. 'Charlie Markleson,' she whispered.

Banks checked the sheet. 'Charles Christopher Markleson.'

'How did you find out their names? I haven't heard them in so long.'

'It doesn't matter how we found out. Was Gloria having an affair with Brad Szikorski when Matthew came back?'

'I don't know what you're getting at. You've been misinformed, Chief Inspector. Gloria was married to Matthew, whether he was there or not. Yes, we went to the pictures and dances with those boys on occasion, but that's all there was to it.'

'How did Gloria behave when she thought her husband was dead. Surely an attractive woman like her must have had boyfriends?'

Vivian paused again. 'Gloria had a very gregarious side to her nature. She liked parties, group excursions, that sort of thing. She liked to keep things superficial. You must understand, Chief Inspector, we never gave up hope that Matthew would return.'

'You haven't answered my question. Did Gloria have a romantic affair with Brad Szikorski, or with anyone else?'

She looked away. 'Not that I knew about.'

'How did Brad take it when Matthew came back alive?'

'How should I know? Why would it matter to him?'

'It might have. If he fell in love with Gloria, and if she rejected him in favour of her husband.'

'Are you suggesting that *Brad* killed Gloria?' Vivian sniffed.

Banks leaned forward. 'Somebody did, Ms Elmsley, and the most immediate suspects that come to mind are Matthew, one of the Americans, Michael Stanhope, or you.'

'Ridiculous. It must have been a stranger.'

'You must see how the discovery casts suspicion on your

brother, most of all. Gloria was buried in an outbuilding adjoining Bridge Cottage. Matthew was living with her there at the time.'

'But I had never known him be violent. Never.'

'War can change a man.'

'Even so.'

'Did he go out much after his return. Was Gloria often alone in the house?'

'He went to the pub of an evening. The Shoulder of Mutton. Yes, she was alone there sometimes.'

'Would it surprise you to hear that Gloria posed nude for a painting by Stanhope in 1944?'

'Yes, it would. Very much.'

'Was Gloria having an affair with Michael Stanhope?'

'I shouldn't think so. He was too old for her.'

'And homosexual?'

'I wouldn't know about that. I was very young.'

'Did she ever tell you about her son, Francis?'

'She did mention him to me once, yes. But she said she'd cut off all relations with him and his father.'

'There is one thing that really puzzles me,' Banks said, 'and that's what you *did* think had happened to Gloria? Surely you can't have thought she had simply disappeared from the face of the earth?'

'It wasn't a mystery at the time. Not really. She left because she couldn't stand it any more, taking care of Matthew, the way he was. After all, it wouldn't have been the first time she'd run away. She had clearly broken off all contact with whatever life she had had in London before coming to Hobb's End.'

'When did she disappear?' he asked.

'Shortly after V-E Day. A week or so. I had accompanied Matthew to his doctor in Leeds. When we got back that evening, she was gone.'

'Did Gloria ever say anything to you about leaving?'

'She hinted at it once or twice, but I didn't take her seriously. It was as if she was joking. You know, "Some day my prince will come. I'm going to leave all this behind and run off to untold wealth and riches." Gloria was a dreamer, Chief Inspector.'

'Did she take anything with her when she left?'

'A few clothes, personal items. She didn't have much.'

'That's interesting. What did she carry them in?'

'An old cardboard suitcase. The same one she arrived with.'

Banks paused. 'Ms Elmsley,' he asked, 'knowing what you know now, where do you think her clothes and suitcase got to?'

'I have no idea. I'm only telling you what I thought must have happened at the time. Perhaps someone stole them. To make it *look* as if she had gone away.'

'Ah. And who do you think would feel the need to risk taking time burying her body under the outbuilding floor?'

'Someone who wanted to avoid suspicion.'

'Exactly. Which brings us back very close to home, doesn't it? Why try to avoid suspicion? It had to be someone who felt suspicion was likely to fall on him or her: Matthew, Brad Szikorski or *you*.'

'Well, it wasn't me. And I told you, Matthew never raised a finger to her.'

'Which leaves Brad Szikorski.'

'Perhaps. Though I doubt it. Anyway Brad Szikorski was killed in a flying stunt in the desert outside Los Angeles in 1952.'

'What about Charles Markleson?'

'Charlie was killed in the war.'

'Edgar Konig? Billy Joe Farrell?'

'I don't know what happened to them, Chief Inspector.'

'Had either of them reason to kill Gloria?'

'Not that I know of. Though Billy Joe, I remember, did have a violent temper, and PX was rather smitten with Gloria.'

'Did she go out with him?'

'Not to my knowledge. He . . . He just seemed so *young* and shy.'

'Did you notice any blood in Bridge Cottage following Gloria's disappearance?'

'No. Obviously, if I had done, I would have been suspicious and called the police. Anyway, what makes you think she was killed in Bridge Cottage? She could have been killed outside, in the back yard, or even in the outbuilding.'

'Possibly,' Banks allowed. 'What happened next?'

'Nothing. We just carried on. Actually, we only stayed on in the village a few weeks longer, then we got a council house in Leeds.'

'What about Matthew? Did you kill him?'

'I did not. He committed suicide.'

'Why?'

'It wasn't related to Gloria's disappearance. He was ill, confused, depressed, in pain. I did my best for him, but it was no use.'

'He shot himself, didn't he?'

'Yes.'

'Where did he get the gun?'

'He always had it.'

'Always? Since when?'

'I don't know. Since he came back from the war, I suppose.'

'From the Japanese POW camp?'

'Yes.'

Banks got to his feet, shaking his head.

'What's wrong, Chief Inspector?' Vivian asked.

'Everything,' said Banks. 'Your brother Matthew shot himself with an American service revolver he just happened to bring back from a Japanese POW camp? *You* write detective novels. Ask yourself if your Inspector Niven would believe it. Ask yourself if your readers would believe it.' He reached in his pocket. 'Here's my card. I want you to think seriously about our little talk. We'll be back. Soon.'

Once they were out in the street again, Annie turned to Banks, whistled and said, 'She was lying.'

'Of course she was.' Banks looked at his watch. 'Want to grab a bite to eat?'

'Yes. I'm starving.'

They found a small café and Annie had a Greek salad, while Banks went for the prosciutto sandwich.

'But why was she lying?' Annie asked. 'I don't get it.'

'She's protecting herself. Or someone else.'

'So what do we do now?'

'Nothing,' said Banks. 'Leave her to stew overnight. I get the impression she has a lot on her conscience. If I'm right, she's near the end of her tether on this. We'll have another go at her tomorrow.'

'And in the meantime?'

'First, we'll go and see if we can find Francis Henderson. And then if it's OK with you, I'd like to head out to Bethnal Green and see my son. We've got a few things to talk over.'

'Of course. I understand. Maybe I'll go to the pictures. What about later?'

'Remember that naughty weekend you mentioned?'

Annie nodded.

'I don't know if you're still interested, but there's this discreet little hotel in Bloomsbury. And it *is* Friday. Even CID get to work regular hours sometimes.'

Annie blushed. 'But I didn't bring my toothbrush.'

Banks laughed. 'I'll buy you one.'

'Last of the big spenders.' The corner of her mouth twitched in a smile. 'And I didn't bring my nightie, either.'

'Don't worry,' said Banks. 'You won't need your nightie.'

OVER THE NEXT couple of weeks, as I continued to mourn Charlie, I noticed no improvement in Matthew's condition. He remained at Bridge Cottage with Gloria. I don't really think it mattered to him *where* he was, as long as his basic creature comforts were taken care of. There wasn't a day went by when I didn't spend time sitting with him, talking to him, though he never responded.

We soon got Matthew fixed up with Dr Jennings, a psychiatrist at Leeds University. Once a week, Gloria or I would take him to his appointment, spend an hour or so looking round the shops, then collect him and take him home. Dr Jennings admitted to me on the third visit that he was having little success and was considering narcosynthesis, despite the problems.

Matthew wasn't any trouble; he just wasn't there. He did, however, get into the habit of going to the Shoulder of Mutton every night and sitting alone in a corner drinking. At first, friends and neighbours who knew him would approach and ask how he was doing, but soon they left him alone. Once in a while he would have an angry outburst and smash a glass or kick a chair. But these were infrequent and soon passed over.

Gloria gave me a key, so I was able to pop in and out of Bridge Cottage whenever I could. She took as much time off from the farm as possible, of course, but she needed the income, and I don't think she could have borne the pain and heartbreak of being with him twenty-four hours a day.

You could smell victory in the air. The Americans had crossed the Rhine, and so had Monty's men. The Russians had Berlin surrounded. In April and May we started hearing the first rumours about concentration camps and atrocities on a scale that had only been hinted at. All the newspapers seemed at a loss as to how to describe what the liberating armies had found at places such as Belsen and Buchenwald. I also read about the appalling tortures inflicted on prisoners like Matthew.

BANKS WALKED into the cavernous East London Victorian pub, all smoked and etched glass, brass fittings and mirrors.

He and Annie had just been to Dulwich to see Francis Henderson, only to find that he was out. A neighbour told them she thought he had most likely gone on holiday, as he had cancelled his newspapers and milk. Banks slipped his card with a note through the letterbox and left it at that.

It was half past five, and the band was due to start at six to draw in the after-work crowd. Brian stood on the low wooden stage along with the others who were setting their equipment up.

He waved Banks over. Brian looked a little nervous, but that was only to be expected; his mates would no doubt tease him about his old man coming to a gig. He introduced Banks to Andy, the keyboard player, Jamisse, the bassist, who was from Mozambique, and the percussionist, Ali.

'I've just got to tune up,' said Brian, 'then I'll come over.'

'Fine. Pint?'

'Sure.'

Banks bought a couple of pints at the bar and found an empty table. Occasionally, feedback screeched from the amps, Ali hit a snare drum or Jamisse plucked at a bass string. It was a quarter to six when Brian detached himself from the others and came over. Tall and skinny, he wore threadbare jeans, trainers and a plain red T-shirt. His dark hair was long and straight, and he had three or four days' growth around his chin. He sat down and scratched his cheek, avoiding Banks's eyes.

Banks didn't want to launch right into the midst of things. 'I'm looking forward to this,' he said, nodding towards the stage. 'I haven't heard you play since you used to practise at home.'

'I hope I've got better since then, Dad.'

'Me, too.' Banks smiled. 'Cheers.' They clinked glasses, then Banks lit a cigarette. 'What kind of music do you play?'

'You'll have to wait and hear it for yourself. I can't describe it.'

'Blues?'

'Not straight blues, no. I write most of the lyrics, Jamisse does most of the music. Andy can read music, so he arranges and stuff. We do some cover versions, too.'

'Anything an old fogey like me would recognise?'

Brian grinned. 'You might be surprised. Got to go now. Will you be around after?'

Banks looked at his watch. Six. Plenty of time. 'I don't have to leave until about eight,' he said.

'Great.'

The next thing Banks knew, the band had started. There was blues underlying the music, definitely. Andy's ghostly keyboards floated around it all, and Brian's guitar cut through the rhythms clear as a bell. When he soloed, which he did very well, the sound reminded Banks of early Jerry Garcia and Eric Clapton. There was an improvisational, jazzy element to the music, but it was accessible, *popular*.

Then the first set ended. The band acknowledged the applause, then Brian came over. Banks bought them both another pint.

'That was great,' Banks said.

Brian glanced away. 'Thanks.'

There was no point in putting it off any longer, Banks thought, taking a deep breath. 'Look,' he said, 'about what we said on the phone the other day. I'm disappointed, of course I am, but it's your life. If you think you can really make a go of this, I'm certainly not going to stand in your way.'

Brian met Banks's gaze, and Banks thought he could see relief in his son's eyes. So his approval *did* matter, after all.

'You mean it?'

Banks nodded.

'Architecture was just so boring, Dad. I'm sorry if I caused you any grief. But it was only partly because of the band. I didn't do enough work last year because I was bored by the whole subject.'

'Have you told your mother yet?'

'I left a message on her machine.'

'Look, when you get a bit of free time, why don't you come up to Gratly? You haven't even seen the cottage yet. We can go for long walks together, the way we used to. I'm not asking you to put a date to it. It's an open invitation. OK?'

Brian looked up from his beer and smiled. 'OK,' he said. 'I'd like that. It's a deal.'

ONE DAY GLORIA ASKED if I would mind closing the shop for an hour or so and walking with her. She looked pale and hadn't taken her usual pains with her appearance.

It was the beginning of May, I remember. Hitler was dead, the Russians had Berlin, and all the German troops in Italy had surrendered. It could only be days from the end now.

I closed the shop and we walked into Rowan Woods, wandering in the filtered green light of the new leaves. The woodland flowers were all in bloom, clusters of bluebells here and there, violets and primroses. Birds were singing and the air was pungent with the smell of wild garlic.

'I don't know what to do with him, Gwen,' she said, close to tears. 'Nothing I do to try to reach him does any good.'

'I know,' I said. 'We just have to be patient.' Even as I spoke I felt the inadequacy of my words.

'It's all right for you. He's not your husband. It's not the same. I'm living with a stranger. I don't know what to do. Brad is still pestering me to run off back to America with him. Just imagine it, Gwen: Hollywood! A new life in the sunshine. A young, healthy, handsome, vigorous man who dotes on me . . .'

'But?'

She turned away, eyes downcast. 'A dream. That's all. I can't go. Silly, isn't it? A few years ago I did exactly that. Walked away from a life I didn't want and ended up here.'

'But you'd lost your whole family then. You had nothing to stay for. Anyone can understand your doing that.'

'But I'd walked away even before I lost them.'

'What do you mean?'

She paused. 'There are things you don't know about me, Gwen. I've been selfish. I've hurt people. But I want you to know that Matt

is the only man I have ever truly loved. Not Brad, not . . . Never mind.'

'What were you going to say?'

Gloria paused and looked at me with those blue eyes of hers. 'I won't ask you to forgive me,' she said. 'You might not be able to do that. But at least hear me out.'

I nodded. She leaned back against a tree.

'When I was sixteen,' she began, 'I had a baby. I didn't love the father, not really. I was infatuated. George was good-looking, popular with all the girls. I was flattered by his attentions. We only did it once, but I didn't know about . . . you know . . . then, and I got pregnant. George would have married me like a shot—he said he loved me—but I *knew* deep down that it would be the worst mistake of my life. I knew if I married George I would be unhappy. He drank, like they all did down on the docks, and I really believed it was just a matter of time before he would start beating me.'

'But what about the baby?'

'After I had Francis I got very depressed and I didn't . . . I didn't feel what they said a normal mother should. I'm ashamed to say it, but I hated my own baby, Gwen. That's why I could never be a real mother to him or to anyone else.'

She sobbed and fell forward into my arms. I held her and comforted her as best I could. Sniffling, dabbing her handkerchief to her eyes, Gloria went on, 'George's sister Ivy couldn't have any children of her own. She and her husband are decent people. They'd got away and bettered themselves. They said they would take care of Francis. I knew he would be better off with them.'

'What did George say?'

'He couldn't understand it when I didn't object to giving up Francis to Ivy and John. He said that a boy needed a real mother to love. But, of course, he agreed. He could hardly bring up Francis on his own. He wasn't a bad man. It's me who's bad. I think he loved his son more than I did. He wanted to be a father as much as he could. But he got called up, of course. Anyway, he always thought I would change my mind. He's already been up to see me once with Francis. He said he still loves me, urged me to go back. I told him I was married and we had an argument.'

I didn't know what to say.

'Say you don't hate me, Gwen, please! I couldn't bear it if you hated me. You're my only real friend.'

'Of course I don't hate you. I just don't understand.'

'I don't know if I do, either, but don't you see that's exactly why I *can't* leave Matt? Because of what I did before. This is my punishment, Gwen. Don't you see? Matt is my penance.'

'I think so,' I said. 'Are you and Brad still . . .?'

'Sometimes. Don't be angry. Brad brings me comfort from time to time and as long as Matt doesn't know . . . To be honest, though, he's more trouble than he's worth right now. I just can't keep him off the subject of running away together. It's all getting to be too much of a strain. I told him if he didn't stop pushing me I'd run off and leave the whole lot of you behind, him included.'

'Have you had any more trouble from Billy Joe?'

'No, not really. I got the impression he was secretly pleased that Matt had come back and spoilt things for me and Brad. I don't think he gives a damn about what it's all doing to *me*. Look, Gwen, I don't know if I should be telling you this, but I've been having a few problems with Michael.'

'Michael? Good Lord. You don't mean he's—'

'Don't be a fool, Gwen. The man's only interested in boys. No. But, last summer and autumn, you might have noticed I spent quite a bit of time at his studio. He was painting me.'

'But that's wonderful, Gloria. Can I see it? Is it finished?'

'Yes. And it's very good. It's a nude.'

I swallowed. 'You posed in the *nude* for Michael Stanhope?'

She laughed. 'Why not? There certainly wasn't much chance of him trying to put his hands on me, was there? Anyway, the point is, I begged him not to exhibit it, as long as Matthew is alive. I just don't know how it would affect him. Who knows if seeing a nude painting of his wife won't send him right over the edge?'

'That sounds reasonable,' I told her. 'What did Michael Stanhope have to say?'

'Oh, he's not happy about it. Thinks it's one of the best things he's done, blah blah. Says his career needs a boost and this could give it one. But he agreed in the end. He likes to play the miserable cynic, but he's pretty decent, deep down.'

There she finished and we walked back to Hobb's End enjoying the

sound of the breeze through the leaves and the songs of the birds in the high branches.

I didn't see Gloria again until a couple of days later, and by then everyone knew Germany had surrendered. The war was over.

'ENJOY THE FILM?' Banks asked, when he met Annie outside the Leicester Square Odeon at nine o'clock. She had been to see the latest megamillion special-effects extravaganza.

'Not much,' said Annie. 'I suppose it had its good points.'

'What?'

'*The End*, for one.'

Banks laughed.

'How were things with your son?' Annie asked.

'We mended a bridge or two.'

He took Annie to a small bistro-style restaurant just off Shaftesbury Avenue. The place was busy, but they managed to get a table after a short wait.

They chose a claret and Banks went for roast lamb with rosemary, while Annie settled for a green salad and some bread and cheese.

Their food arrived more quickly than Banks expected, and they paused until the waiter had gone. Beyond the hum of conversation, clinking of cutlery and glassware, Banks could hear Tchaikovski's 'String Quartet No. 1' playing in the background.

After his talk with Brian, he felt as if a burden had been lifted from his mind. He and his son were talking again. And from what he had heard, the kid had talent; he might make it in the business yet.

The candlelight brought out the slight wine flush on Annie's cheeks and filled her dark eyes with mysterious reflections. Her hair tumbled over her shoulders in sexy waves.

'What are you thinking about?' she asked, looking up.

Perhaps this was the moment, Banks thought, emboldened by his buoyant mood. 'Annie, can I ask you a personal question?'

She arched her eyebrows and Banks sensed a part of her scurry back into the shadows. Too late now. 'Of course,' she said. 'But I can't promise to answer it.'

'Fair enough. What are you doing at Harkside? It's a nowhere posting. You're bright. You've got a future ahead of you if you want it, but you'll not get the job experience you need at Harkside.'

'I think that's rather insulting to Inspector Harmond and the others up there, don't you?'

'Oh, come on, Annie. You know as well as I do that's where they want to be. They chose the easy life.'

'Well, maybe it's what I've chosen, too.'

'Is it?'

'I didn't promise to answer your question.' Her mouth took on a sulky cast Banks hadn't seen before.

'No, you didn't,' Banks said, leaning towards her. 'But let me tell you something. Jimmy Riddle hates my guts. He isn't in the business of putting me in the way of anything I might find even remotely pleasant. The only reason I'm asking you now is because . . . because I'm afraid you're being used, too. Riddle had to have a reason for putting us together, something he thought would be unpleasant for me.'

She tilted her head. 'Perhaps this is it?' Annie suggested. 'What he expected. That we'd get together somehow, break the rules and get caught. That way he could be rid of both of us.'

'No, that's too easy. What we're doing isn't . . . I mean, it's only the same kind of thing he thought I was doing before. He has a far more sadistic mind than that.'

Annie shook her head slowly and then she seemed to come to some kind of decision. She looked at Banks. 'All right,' she said. 'I'll tell you, but only if you'll tell me something, too.'

On May 8, 1945, it poured down all morning, despite the fact that this was V-E Day. By early afternoon, the rain was tapering off and we were left with as beautiful a warm May evening as you could ever ask for, the grass green and moist from the rain.

Gloria gave me a pair of stockings she had got from PX, and helped me with my make-up. First, we spent an hour or so at the Hobb's End street party. People had brought little tables and put them together in a row all along the High Street. It was a dull affair, though, as there were so few people left in the village.

Mother sat at one of the tables with her friend, Joyce Maddingley,

and she told us to behave ourselves when we slipped away to the celebration dance at Harkside. Matthew refused to come out of the cottage at all. Mother said she would look in on him.

From the minute we got to Harkside village green, we were swept into a mad whirl. Most of the soldiers and airmen from the nearby bases had come. It didn't take Gloria long to meet up with Brad. Billy Joe was there with his new girlfriend, and PX was tagging along, too. I felt a sudden pang of missing Charlie, then I tried to enter into the spirit of victory.

First we went to the dance at the Mechanics Institute. There was a big band playing Glenn Miller, Duke Ellington and Benny Goodman tunes, and people kept throwing coloured streamers across the dance floor. At one point, I noticed Gloria and Brad slip outside. It was over an hour before I saw them again, and Gloria had retouched her make-up. I resolved to say nothing. I had thought a lot about Gloria and what she was sacrificing to care for Matthew, and I decided that she deserved her little pleasures.

The band was still playing when we piled out into the street. There was a huge bonfire on the village green and people were singing and setting off fireworks. The air was full of the acrid smell of smoke and the sky full of exploding colours. Everyone was drunk. I could see Gloria and Brad through the flames having an argument.

At one point we went to someone's house and drank some whisky. It was a wild party. People were packed in like sardines and the house was full of smoke. Gloria was dancing, but I couldn't see Brad. PX was drunk, and I saw him try to kiss a woman. She pushed him away and his face turned red. Then he stormed off. It was almost one o'clock when I told Gloria it was time for us to go.

The two of us were a little drunk. It was on emotion and excitement as much as alcohol. We danced and laughed our way home.

Bridge Cottage was dark. I went in with Gloria to make sure everything was all right and we heard Matthew snoring on the chesterfield. Gloria gestured me towards the kitchen. She poured us both another whisky, which was probably the last thing we needed. When she put her handbag on the countertop, it slipped off and fell on the floor. I bent over to pick it up and noticed how heavy it was. Curious, I opened the clasp and nearly fainted when I saw a gun.

Gloria turned.

'You weren't supposed to see that.'

'But, Gloria, where did you get it?'

'From one of the Americans at the party. He was so drunk he won't miss it.'

'What do you want a gun for?'

She shrugged. 'I just feel more comfortable knowing it's there, that's all.'

'But Matthew's harmless. He wouldn't hurt you.'

She looked at me as if I were the biggest fool she had ever met. 'Who said anything about Matthew?' she said, then took the gun and put it in one of the kitchen cupboards behind the tea and cocoa. 'Now will you have that drink?'

VIVIAN ELMSLEY was having a difficult time. Close to midnight she was sitting in her sparse living room, her third gin and tonic in her hand and some dreadful rubbish on television. Sleep refused to come. Chief Inspector Banks knew she was lying; nobody who had been as close to the people involved as she had been could know as little as she had professed.

Why *hadn't* she told them the truth? She didn't want to go to jail. But would they really prosecute her after so long? Were there not mitigating circumstances? She didn't know what they would do, and that was the problem. On the other hand, if she didn't tell them, then they would never find out the truth. Nobody else knew.

Only one thing was certain: the police would be back. Tonight she had to make her decision.

'YOU'RE RIGHT about one thing,' Annie began. 'I'm in Harkside because I was a naughty girl.'

'What happened?'

'Depends on your point of view. Look, I'm not going to tell you where it was or who was involved. OK?'

'OK. Go on.'

'This is hard.'

'You don't have to.'

She held up her hand. 'No. I've come this far.' She played with a spoon. 'It was when I made DS,' she said. 'Nearly two years ago now. There was a celebration at the local coppers' pub. The private room upstairs. I suppose I was dead chuffed with myself. I'd always wanted to be one of the boys. It got down to just four of us left. One of them suggested we go back to his place and drink some more.'

She was speaking very quietly so that no one would hear. Banks had to strain to hear her.

'We were already three sheets to the wind,' Annie went on, 'and I was the only female. I didn't know the others well. Things were getting pretty wild. I suppose I should have known what was coming by the way the conversation was going. But I'd been drinking, too, and I didn't really think much of it until one of them suggested we go in the bedroom, said he could tell I'd been wanting it all night. I laughed and brushed him off. I thought he was joking. He got angry. Things got out of hand. The other two grabbed me and held me down over the back of the settee while he raped me.'

Annie took a deep breath and went on. 'When he'd finished, they started rearranging positions, and I knew what was coming, so I slipped free, kicked the one who'd raped me as hard as I could in the balls and caught another on the jaw with my elbow. I managed to make it to the door. The third one caught me, and by then the one I'd hit with my elbow was up again. They were mad as hell. One of them punched me in the stomach and I went down. I thought they were going to do what they'd intended, but they'd lost their bottle. Suddenly they were individuals again, each looking out for number one, and they knew what they'd done. They told me to get out. I left.'

'Did you report it? For crying out loud, Annie, you'd been *raped.*'

She shook her head. 'You know what I did? I walked the city most of the night in a complete daze. I remember trying to feel some sort of emotion. There was nothing. Just a deep, cold numbness. When I finally found myself back at my flat, I had a long hot bath. Hours I must have lain there, just listening to the radio. That was soothing somehow. And do you know what? I understand every one of those rape victims who never comes forward to report the crime.'

Banks could see tears glistening at the corners of her eyes.

'What happened?' he asked.

'By morning I'd got a bit of nerve back. I went to see the chief super to tell him what they did. Two of the others had got there before me. Pre-emptive strike. They told the super there'd been a spot of bother at a party last night, just an initiation rite that got a bit out of hand, nothing serious, like, but that I'd probably be coming to complain, making up all sorts of wild allegations.'

'And he believed them?'

'Their word against mine. Besides, people around the station already thought I was a bit weird. You know, I did yoga and meditation and I didn't eat meat. I also had a reputation for not being very interested in men. As it happened, I did have a boyfriend at the time, but I kept my private life separate from the job.'

'Did you tell the chief super what really happened?'

'Yes. Every detail. He looked very embarrassed.'

'Didn't he initiate some sort of inquiry?'

'Like I said, their word against mine. And apart from a pair of torn knickers, I'd pretty much destroyed the evidence, hadn't I? The chief super also told me that that sort of internal investigation hurts everyone, especially the force. He said the officers involved would be disciplined for their excessive high spirits, but it would be best for all concerned if it went no further than his office.'

'He should have been kicked off the force.'

'I'm glad you agree.'

'So all that happened was they got a slap on the wrist.'

'Not quite.' Annie looked down into her coffee cup. 'There were complications.' She stared down for a few more seconds before looking up at Banks. 'Remember, I told you I kicked one of them? Something went wrong. They had to operate. He'd only been married a year. Planning a family.'

'Jesus. I can imagine you were popular after that.'

'Exactly. The chief superintendent suggested it might be better for all concerned if I transferred somewhere else, and they came up with Harkside. I think that our ACC used to work with Chief Constable Riddle, so Riddle knows all about what happened.'

'Which means that to him you're a real troublemaker? A ball-busting lesbian bitch?'

Annie mustered a crooked smile.

'No wonder Riddle put us together. I'm sorry about what happened to you, Annie. Sorrier than I can say. I'm also amazed you would even consider getting involved with me. I would have thought that what happened would have been enough to put you off your fellow coppers for life.'

'Oh, Alan. You do yourself a disservice. I've never seen any similarity between you and the men who assaulted me. I wanted you. I was terrified, but I wanted to overcome my fear. The thing is, I thought I'd faced up to it and got on with my life.'

'Haven't you? You seem to be doing all right to me.'

'I thought I was over it but I've been in hiding at Harkside. I get by. I have my nice, safe little life. I go to work, I do my job, and then I come home. No social life.' She paused. 'Let's face it, I know I'm good at the job but I haven't done any serious detective work in Harkside, until this case came along.'

'And now?'

She shrugged. 'I don't know. You're the first person I've told. Now it's your turn. You promised to tell me something, too.'

'Did I? What do you want to know?'

'Did you really punch Jimmy Riddle?'

Banks stubbed out his cigarette and slipped his credit card on the tray the waiter had left. It was snatched up almost immediately.

'Yes,' he said. 'I did.'

She laughed. 'Bloody hell. I wish I'd been there.'

Banks signed the receipt, then they walked out into the busy West End evening. The streets were packed with people standing drinking outside the pubs.

As they turned onto Great Russell Street, Annie slipped her arm through Banks's. It was only the second time they had had any intimate physical contact in public, and it felt good. Annie rested her head on his shoulder; her hair tickled his cheek.

They passed the dark mass of the British Museum, set back behind its railings and courtyard, then crossed Russell Square.

'Here we are,' said Banks. 'Did you buy a toothbrush?'

'Yup.' Annie held up a bag. 'And a nightie.'

'I thought I said you wouldn't need one.'

She laughed and moved closer. 'Oh, don't worry. It's only a *little* nightie. I promise you'll like it.' And they walked up the stone steps.

I COULDN'T STOP thinking about the gun. Usually, the way the scene ran in my mind was that Gloria shot Matthew first and then herself. The images were so vivid I could even see the blood gush from their wounds. Finally, I determined I had to do something.

So the next time it was Gloria's turn to take Matthew to Leeds, I let myself in to Bridge Cottage.

I found the gun in the same place Gloria had left it in the kitchen cupboard. I put it in the shopping bag I had brought with me, put the cupboard back in order and left. The best I could hope for was that by the time she missed it she wouldn't feel the need for it any more and would realise what a favour I had done her.

Chapter Eight

It was about eleven o'clock on Saturday morning when Banks and Annie arrived back at Vivian Elmsley's building. Before Banks could even press the buzzer, the street door opened and Vivian almost bumped into them.

'You?' She exclaimed, putting her hand to her heart. 'I didn't think . . . So soon . . . I was just . . . You'd better come in.'

They followed her upstairs to the flat. She was carrying a large buff envelope. Banks glanced at it and saw his name on it.

She turned to face them as they entered her living room. 'You've saved me the postage.'

'What were you sending me?' Banks asked. 'A confession?'

'Of sorts. Yes. I suppose you could call it that.'

'So you *were* lying yesterday?'

'Fiction's my trade. Sometimes I can't help it. Anyway,' she went on, handing Banks the envelope, 'I'd like you to take this away with you and read it. I'm not going to run anywhere, I promise you.'

'Why the change of heart?'

'Conscience, would you believe? I thought I could live with it, but I can't. The telephone calls didn't help, either. I've decided to tell the truth. I'd rather do things this way than answer a lot of questions, and I think it will help you understand. Of course, you'll have questions eventually. I have to be in Leeds next week, so you'll soon have the opportunity. Will you allow me this much, at least?'

If Banks were to go by the book, he wouldn't let a murder suspect hand him a written 'confession', then go away. But it was time for a judgment call. He believed that Vivian Elmsley wasn't going anywhere. She was in the public eye, and he didn't think she had anywhere to run, even if she wanted to. The other possibility was suicide. It was a risk, to be certain, but he decided to take it.

'You mentioned telephone calls,' he said. 'What do you mean?'

'Anonymous calls. Sometimes he says things, other times he just hangs up. He sounds vaguely threatening. And he calls me Gwen Shackleton.'

'Have you any idea who it might be?'

'No. The voice sounds muffled, as if he's speaking through a handkerchief or something.'

'I honestly wouldn't worry too much. In most cases people who make threatening phone calls don't confront their victims. But you should get in touch with your local police station. They'll be able to help.' Banks held up the envelope. 'We'll do as you ask,' he said, 'but how do we know this is the truth and not just more fiction?'

'It's a bit of both, but the parts you'll be interested in are true. You'll just have to take my word for it, won't you?'

THE DAY IT HAPPENED began like any ordinary day; I opened the shop, made lunch and tea for Mother and settled down to an evening's reading and the wireless. The Americans were having a farewell party up at the base that night, as they had heard they would be moving out in a matter of days. Neither Gloria nor I had felt like going. Somehow, that part of our lives seemed over. Charlie was dead and Gloria had made it clear to Brad, after their last fling on V-E Day, that it would be best if they didn't see each other any more.

I wouldn't normally have gone to Bridge Cottage so late in the evening except that Cynthia Garmen had dropped off some parachute silk. I thought Gloria might appreciate a small gift; she had been very depressed since V-E Day. I can't say that I heard any small

voice telling me to go; nor can I recollect any feeling of apprehension. I thought the prospect of making a new dress might cheer Gloria up.

It was just after ten o'clock and Mother had gone to bed. I assumed Matthew would still be at the Shoulder of Mutton, so I thought I would call in there first and persuade him to walk home with me. As it turned out, he had been asked to leave a little earlier because he had had one of his outbursts and broken a glass.

I walked down the dark, deserted High Street to Bridge Cottage. There was light showing between the curtains. I knocked at the door but no one answered. I knocked again. Still nothing. I put my key in the lock, turned it and entered, calling out Gloria's name.

There was no one in the living room but I noticed a strong smell of whisky. I thought I heard a movement in the kitchen. Puzzled, I walked over and when I got to the doorway I saw her.

Gloria lay on the flagstone floor, legs and arms splayed at awkward angles. One of her little fists was curled tight, as if she were about to hit someone, except for the little finger, which stuck out.

I remember being surprised at how little blood there was. Her royal-blue dress was stained with it all over, yet very little had flowed to the floor. Not far from her body lay a broken whisky bottle. Bourbon. An unopened carton of Lucky Strikes sat on the countertop. Above it, the cupboard was open and tea and cocoa had spilt all over the counter and the floor nearby.

Kneeling beside her, holding a bloody kitchen knife, was Matthew. I went over to him, took the knife gently out of his hand and led him through to his armchair. He accompanied me meekly and flopped back in the chair.

'Matthew, what happened? What have you done? You've got to tell me. Why did you do it?'

I gave him pencil and paper, but he just drew in on himself and I could get nothing out of him.

In the end I gave up and went back to the kitchen. I wasn't thinking clearly. I suppose if I assumed anything at all it was that someone must have told him about what his wife got up to while he was out, and that one way or the other it had set off the explosion that had been building in him. Now Gloria was dead.

My heart wept for her; I had come to love her almost as much as I loved Matthew. But there was nothing I could do for her. It didn't matter now what happened to her. Or so I told myself. All I could think about was to protect Matthew. If anyone found out about this, he might be hanged, or, more likely, found insane and put in the lunatic asylum. I knew he wouldn't be able to bear that. I would have to care for him from now on.

The blackout cloth was still rolled up below the windows, where it had been left after I helped Gloria take it down a couple of months before. I gently rolled Gloria onto it, then wrapped it round her as tightly as a shroud. Before I had finished I kissed her on the forehead and said, 'Goodbye, sweet Gloria. Goodbye.' She was still warm.

Where could I hide her? The only place I could think of was the old outbuilding. In the light of a small oil lamp I started to dig the hole. I couldn't manage more than about three feet. I went back to the house, where Matthew hadn't moved, and managed to drag out the roll of blackout cloth and drop it in the hole. There was no one around. Only the black night sky with its uncaring stars.

With tears running down my cheeks, I shovelled the earth back. Some heavy stone slabs stood propped against the wall and I levered them down on top of the makeshift grave. It was the best I could do.

In the house, I swept up the broken glass, the spilt tea leaves and cocoa powder, and put the tins back in the cupboard. As I said, there was very little blood and I scrubbed it off the floor easily enough.

I had to explain where Gloria had gone, so after I had managed to lead Matthew upstairs and put him to bed, I packed his bloody shirt and trousers in a small suitcase and added Gloria's favourite clothes. Then I put her personal odds and ends in too. I wrote a note—Gloria's childlike handwriting and style were easy to imitate. After that, carrying the suitcase, I took the back way to the shop. Matthew didn't seem aware of what was happening and I had no idea whether he would remember what he had done.

Early the next day I went back to Bridge Cottage, found Matthew still in bed, 'found' the note and proceeded to tell everyone we knew that Gloria had run away during the night because she couldn't bear her life with Matthew any more. She said she loved him, but she couldn't be responsible for her actions if she stayed. Then I showed them the note, which said exactly that. She ended by saying that we shouldn't go looking for her because we would never be able to find her. Everyone believed the note without question.

I gave up Bridge Cottage, sold the contents and brought Matthew to live with us above the shop.

One evening when Mother was at Joyce Maddingley's, I took Matthew's bloodstained clothes and Gloria's dresses and burned them in the grate. I disposed of her trinkets in Leeds the next time I went there on shop business. I just stood on Leeds Bridge and dropped them one by one into the River Aire.

As I had expected, it was Brad who gave me the most trouble. He just couldn't believe that Gloria had simply left. If she wanted to go, he argued, then why didn't she go with him? He had asked her often enough. I told him I thought she wanted a completely new start. It hurt him deeply, which I hated to do, but he had to accept what I said in the end. The 448th Bomber Group moved out of Rowan Woods and I heard nothing more from Brad.

Michael Stanhope expressed sorrow that such a beautiful spirit had left. He said something about Hobb's End having glimmered briefly, before turning dark again. He was free to sell the nude now, not that I ever heard anything of it again. Perhaps it wasn't as good as he thought it was.

As for Matthew, he went on drinking and staring into space as before. I had to stop the visits to Dr Jennings, of course. Who knew what narcosynthesis might draw out of Matthew?

Soon, we were hearing rumours that the village was to be sold as a reservoir site, and when I looked around it didn't surprise me. I hadn't noticed it happening, but hardly anyone lived there any more. Those who had come back from the war had had a taste of more interesting locales or had been trained for jobs they could only get in the cities. The mill closed. Buildings fell into disrepair. Old people died. Finally, there was nobody left.

One day, before we left for Leeds, a man came into the shop with a little boy of about eight or nine and asked to see Gloria. I knew immediately who they were.

'Are you a relative?' I asked him.

'No,' he said. 'Just an old friend, that's all. I was passing this way, so I thought I'd look her up.' He sounded rather sad, and I noticed he had a cockney accent.

I asked him more questions, to show interest. Most of all, I wanted him to be satisfied by my explanation of Gloria's disappearance. I needn't have worried. When he left, he just said, 'If you do see her again, tell her George and little Frankie dropped by and send their love.'

I assured him I would. The little boy had said nothing at all, but I felt him staring at me the whole time. On impulse, I gave him a quarter of gumdrops. He thanked me solemnly and then they left.

The following week, Matthew, Mother and I moved to Leeds and Hobb's End ceased to exist.

ON SUNDAY MORNING, Annie was lying back in Banks's front room, barefoot, her feet dangling over the arm of the settee, reading about Gwen Shackleton's war.

'It's a confession of sorts, isn't it? she said. 'She does admit to interfering with the body. That makes her an accessory.'

'I very much doubt that any judge would admit the manuscript as evidence. All she has to do is say it's fiction. Any decent lawyer would make mincemeat of it. She makes her living writing detective fiction.' He ran his hand across his head. 'Believe me, the CPS can't even keep up with today's crimes, let alone put staff on prosecuting yesterday's on evidence so flimsy a puff of wind would blow it away.'

'So that's it? We go no further? To be honest, it looks to me as if the poor woman's suffered enough. What a blighted life. She still committed a crime, though.'

'Yes, but she's not the killer.'

'Unless she's lying in the story.'

'I don't think so. She did what she did to protect her brother, who had already suffered terribly in the war. If she'd called the police at the time, it's almost certain he would have been convicted of Gloria's murder. Unless . . .'

'Unless what?'

'Unless he didn't do it. There are a number of things in Gwen's version that bother me. Gwen notices that Gloria's fist is clenched apart from the little finger which appears to be broken. Right?'

'Right.'

'And Gloria's body is still warm. Which means that the clenched fist wasn't caused by rigor mortis; it was caused by a cadaveric spasm. What if the killer, the *real* killer, had been trying to take something out of Gloria's hand when he was disturbed by Matthew coming home? Something that might have incriminated him.'

'The button? It's certainly possible.'

Banks shook his head. 'But they'd still probably have arrested Matthew. The crazy husband would have looked the most obvious suspect, and the button, even if they had found it, could have been explained away.'

'So what do we do next?'

'We could hand the report to Jimmy Riddle and get on with our lives. Or look into those one or two little inconsistencies I mentioned. For a start, I'm not convinced that—'

The doorbell rang.

Banks went to answer the door. Annie heard a woman's voice, then in she walked. Blonde hair, black eyebrows, attractive, good figure, dressed in a pastel skirt and a white blouse. For a moment, she seemed speechless, a slight flush suffusing her pale complexion, then she moved forward and said, 'Hello, I don't think we've been introduced.'

Feeling foolish, Annie stood up. 'Annie Cabbot,' she said.

'Sandra Banks,' said the other. 'Pleased to meet you.'

Banks stood behind them looking uncomfortable. 'DS Cabbot and I were just discussing the Thornfield Reservoir case,' he said. 'Maybe you've read about it?'

Sandra looked down at Annie's bare feet, then gave Banks a withering glance. 'Yes, of course,' she said. 'And on a Sunday morning, too. Such devotion to duty.'

Annie felt herself blush to her roots.

'Anyway,' Banks gibbered on, 'it's really nice to see you. Would you like some coffee or something?'

Sandra shook her head. 'No, I don't think so. I just came up to Eastvale to see to some things. I thought I'd drop by to talk to you about our son, but it'll do some other time. Don't let me interrupt.'

She opened the door and was gone.

Annie stood facing Banks in silence for a few moments, aware only of her fast and loud heartbeat and burning skin. 'I didn't know what to say,' she said. 'I felt foolish, embarrassed.'

'Why? Sandra and I have been separated for almost a year.'

'Yes, I know. It was just a shock, meeting her like that.'

Banks gave a nervous laugh. 'You can say that again. Look, let's sit outside, OK? Put Vivian Elmsley on the back burner for a while. It's a beautiful day, shame to waste it staying indoors.'

'OK.' Annie followed him outside, still feeling dazed. She sat on a striped deck chair. Banks read *The Sunday Times*, trying to pretend everything was just fine, but she knew he was rattled, too. Perhaps even more than she was. After all, he had been married to the woman for more than twenty years.

Annie stared into the distance at Witch Fell, whose massive shape took up most of the western skyline.

'Are you OK?' Banks asked, looking up from his paper.

'Fine,' she said, mustering a smile. 'Fine.'

But she wasn't. She should have known how fleeting happiness was; and what a mistake it is to allow oneself to get too close to anyone. Closeness like that stirs up all the old demons—the jealousy, the insecurity. A shadow had blotted out her sun, just the way Witch Fell obscured the sky.

RAIN HAD FINALLY come to the Dales, and the Golden Grill was almost empty. Doris, the proprietor, claimed Banks and Sergeant Hatchley, who had walked across for toasted tea cakes and coffee, were only the fourth and fifth customers to pass through her door that day.

'Does that put us in line for summat special, like?' Hatchley asked. 'Maybe a free cuppa?'

She slapped his arm and laughed. 'Get away with you.'

'Worth a try,' said Hatchley to Banks. 'Never ask, never get.'

Banks laughed, then he asked, 'Have you heard anything on that nationwide inquiry you put out yet?'

'Something came in this morning, as a matter of fact,' said Hatchley. 'Lass called Brenda Hamilton was found dead in a barn. Strangled and stabbed. In that order.'

'It certainly *sounds* promising.'

Hatchley shook his head. 'Don't get your hopes up. I only mentioned it because it was the same MO. There's a couple of problems. It happened near Hadleigh, Suffolk, in August 1952. That's seven years after Gloria Shackleton was killed. It's a long gap. It also happened in another part of the country.'

'There could be reasons for that.'

'And I doubt there'd be any American air force personnel around by then, would there? I mean the war was long over.'

'You're probably right, Jim, but get onto East Anglia and ask for more details. I'll ask DS Cabbot to contact the Americans again and see if she can find out anything.'

'Will do.'

Back in his office, Banks put off phoning Annie at Harkside, smoking a cigarette instead and staring out of the window. A warm, slow rain fell on the market square, darkening the cobbles. It wasn't bringing much relief; the air was still sticky and humid.

Sunday had gone badly after Sandra's visit, and it annoyed him that he felt that way. After all, *she* had a new boyfriend. Conversation had been awkward, and Annie had eventually left just after lunch, claiming she had things to see to back in Harkside.

At the time, Banks had not been sorry to see her go. He was more upset than he had let on by Sandra's visit. Why did she have to turn up just then, when everything was going so well? What gave her the right to act so shocked that *he* was seeing someone, knocking everyone's feelings out of kilter?

Finally, he plucked up the courage and picked up the phone. 'How's it going?' he asked.

'Fine.'

'You sound distracted.'

'No, I'm not. Just a bit busy. Really. It's fine.'

Banks took a deep breath. 'Look, if it's about Sunday, I'm sorry. I had no idea Sandra was going to turn up.'

'Well, as I said, I'm fine. Except I've got a lot on my plate.'

'OK, if that's how you want to play it. See if you can find out anything about an American air force presence in Suffolk in 1952. And, if there were any bases left, which was the nearest one to Hadleigh.'

'Right.'

'Annie?'

'What?'

'Can't we get together and talk about things?'

'There's nothing to talk about. Really. Look, you know I'm off home on holiday in a couple of days. I've got a lot to do before I go. Maybe when I get back. OK?'

Feeling more depressed than ever, Banks glanced at the pile of paper on his desk: SOCO search results, post-mortem, forensic odontology. None of it told him anything more.

'IT'S JENNY.'

'I know. I recognised your voice. How are you?' said Banks.

'Well, don't sound so excited to hear from me.'

'I'm sorry, Jenny, really. It's just that I'm expecting a call.'

'Well, I won't take up much of your time. I just want to apologise for dumping all over you on our last meeting.'

'What are friends for?'

'Anyway,' Jenny went on, 'by way of an apology, I'd like to invite you to dinner. If you think you can tolerate my cooking, that is?'

'It's bound to be better than mine.'

She laughed a little too nervously. 'How about tomorrow, sevenish?'

'Sounds fine.'

'Are you sure it won't cause any problems?'

'Why should it?'

'I don't know . . . I just . . .' Then her voice brightened. 'That's great. I'll see you tomorrow about seven, then?'

After he hung up, Banks sat back. Dinner with Jenny. At her place. That would be interesting. Then he thought about Annie, and her coldness yesterday, and it cast a shadow over him.

But whatever their personal problems, he *was* anxious to hear from Annie about East Anglia. Shortly before eleven, he did.

'I'm sorry for the delay,' she said. 'What with time differences and faulty fax machines, well, I'm sure you know . . .'

'That's all right. Just tell me what you've discovered.' Banks had already come to one or two conclusions of his own, and he felt the usual tremor of excitement as the pieces started to fall together.

'First off,' Annie said, 'there *was* an American air base near Hadleigh in 1952. The Americans came back in 1948, during the Berlin blockade and airlift. The first thing they did was deploy long-range B-29 bombers from four bases in East Anglia.'

'Any familiar names?'

'Just one. Guess who ran the PX?'

'Edgar Konig.'

'The very same. You don't sound so surprised.'

'Not really. What did you find out about him?'

'He left Rowan Woods in May 1945, and spent some time in Europe, then he returned to America. He was assigned to the base near Hadleigh in summer 1952. Tell me, why doesn't it surprise you? Why not one of the other Americans?'

'The whisky and the Luckies. In Vivian Elmsley's manuscript. She said there was a bottle of whisky smashed on the floor and an *unopened* carton of Lucky Strikes on the kitchen counter.'

'Brad could have brought them.'

'Possible. But it was PX who had access to the stores, PX who always supplied the goodies. The manuscript mentioned a farewell party at Rowan Woods that night. PX must have finally plucked up courage. He'd brought the presents. One last-ditch attempt to buy what he yearned for. Gloria resisted and . . . poor Matthew came in afterwards. Any idea where PX was between 1945 and 1952?'

'No. You're thinking there might be others.'

'Possibly.'

'I can check.'

'Good. See what you can do. I'll talk to you later.'

When Annie had hung up, Banks felt restless. Sometimes waiting was the most difficult part; that was when he smoked too much and paced up and down. There were a couple of things he could do in the meantime. First, he dialled Jenny Fuller's number.

'Alan,' she said. 'Don't tell me you want to cancel?'

'No, no. Actually, I need you to do a little favour for me.'

'Of course. If I can.'

'You said at lunch the other day that you trained with the FBI profilers? Do you have any contacts there? Anyone close enough to ask for a personal favour?'

Jenny paused a moment. 'Well, there is *one* fellow, yes. Why do you ask?'

Banks filled her in on the new developments, then said, 'This Edgar Konig, I'd like you to ask your friend to check his record.

DS Cabbot's working with the military authorities, but any information they can supply us with is limited.'

'I'm sure Bill will be happy to oblige, if he can,' said Jenny.

When Banks had finished giving Jenny the details, he asked DS Hatchley to call East Anglia and find out if a US airman called Edgar Konig had ever been questioned or suspected in connection with the Brenda Hamilton murder.

ON FRIDAY, it was after four o'clock when the publisher's rep dropped Vivian at her Leeds hotel, and the sky looked heavy and dark. In the distance, she could hear hesitant rumbles of thunder and see faint lightning flashes. Even the Metropole's façade, lovingly restored to its original orange terracotta, looked as black as it had when she had stayed there with Charlie all those years ago.

She would have liked nothing better than to rest in her room for an hour or so, perhaps take a long bath. Tomorrow would be taken up with signings in York and Harrogate. She supposed she could put off her trip . . . make the visit on Sunday morning. No. She would not procrastinate. She called the concierge and asked him to arrange for a taxi, then she put on her raincoat and waterproof boots.

Beyond Otley the roads were narrow, and for a while they got stuck behind a lorry doing only about thirty. It was after five o'clock when the driver pulled up in the car park near Thornfield Reservoir. The rain was coming down hard now. Vivian asked the driver to wait.

The path through the woods was treacherous, as if the parched earth had been yearning for the chance to suck up every drop of rain that fell, and Vivian had to be really careful not to slip as she made her way slowly down the embankment.

The ruined village lay spread out before her under the dark sky. Every few seconds a flash of lightning lit the scene.

Vivian paused at the fairy bridge, hardly able to believe that this was the same bridge where she had stood and chatted with Gloria, Matthew, Alice, Cynthia, Betty and the others all those years ago.

She moved towards Bridge Cottage. There was nothing left of the place except the foundations, but she remembered where every room and cupboard had been. The area around and inside the cottage had been dug up. They had been looking for more bodies, Vivian supposed. Well, they would, wouldn't they? Inspector Niven would have done exactly the same thing.

Now, standing there in the driving rain, she was beginning to wonder why she had come. At least when Hobb's End was under water she could imagine it as a place preserved. Now it was exposed as a heap of rubbish and memories, mostly painful. She had in mind only a simple sort of pilgrimage, an acknowledgment of some sort. Well, she had done that. Time to head back.

Lost in her thoughts, she hadn't noticed the gaunt, stringy-haired man who had followed her taxi from Leeds. When she passed Bridge Cottage on her way back, he stepped from behind the outbuilding and held out a gun, then he grabbed her round the throat, and she felt the hard metal pushing at the side of her neck.

Then a dogeared photograph appeared in front of her. It took her a few moments to realise that it was Gloria, perhaps a year or two before she had come to Hobb's End. Rain spattered the photograph and the hand that held it. Such a small hand. *Gloria's hand*, she thought. What was he doing with hands like Gloria's?

BY SIX O'CLOCK on Friday evening, Banks was starting to get nervous about his dinner with Jenny. He had already showered and shaved; now he was trying to decide which version of casual he should put on tonight. It was a decision made a lot easier by the overflowing laundry basket: chinos and a blue denim shirt.

He thought of Annie. Did he owe her fidelity, or were all bets off after the way she had cut him? He didn't know. At the very least, he owed her an explanation of the case. Late that afternoon, Bill Gilchrist of the FBI had sent him, at Jenny's request, a six-page fax on Edgar 'PX' Konig, and Banks had been gobsmacked by its contents. DS Hatchley had also determined that Konig *had* been questioned in connection with the Brenda Hamilton murder.

Annie wasn't at the section station, or at home, when he phoned. He dialled her mobile number but still got no answer.

He was just heading into the bathroom to brush his teeth when the telephone rang.

'Don't you watch the news?' growled Chief Constable Riddle.

'No, sir. I've been getting ready to go out.'

'Then you'd better cancel. I'm calling from Thornfield Reservoir. Shortly over an hour ago, a woman was taken hostage. She had taken a taxi out there and told the driver to wait. When he thought he'd waited long enough, he went to look for her and saw her standing with a man who appeared to be holding a gun to her head. The taxi driver ran back to his car and phoned the police. The woman's name is Vivian Elmsley. Ring any bells?'

Banks's heart lurched. 'Vivian Elmsley? Yes, she's—'

'I know damn well who she is, Banks. What I don't know is why some maniac is holding a gun to her head and demanding to talk to the detective in charge of the Gloria Shackleton investigation.'

'What's his name?'

'He hasn't said. We, however, have gone into full bloody Hollywood production mode out here, with a big enough budget to bankrupt us. A hostage negotiator has spoken with him briefly from a distance. He won't say any more until we get you to the scene. There's an Armed Response Unit here already. Get yourself down here, man. Now!'

When Riddle hung up, Banks reached for his raincoat and shot out of the door.

ANNIE HAD MANAGED to get away from the station early, and by six o'clock she was approaching Blackburn on the M65. It was Friday rush hour; lightning forked and flickered over the humped Pennines, and thunder rumbled and crashed like a mad percussionist in the distance. Annie counted the gaps between the lightning and thunder, wondering if that really *did* tell you how far away the storm was.

What was the gap between her and Banks now? Could it be counted, like that between the thunder and the lightning?

It was all getting to be too much: first, there was the annoyance she had felt when he went out boozing with his mate; then the time he had gone to meet his son and made it clear she wasn't welcome; and then Sandra's appearance on Sunday morning. If every little thing like that was going to rub up against her raw nerve ends, then where would she find any peace?

If she stayed with him, she would have to meet his son and to pass the Dad's-new-girlfriend test. And there would be the divorce, something else they'd have to go through. She didn't think she could face all the emotional detritus of someone else's life impinging on her own.

Annie had the electronic gismo in the car stereo set so that no matter what programme she was listening to, the nearest local station would cut in with its weather and travel updates. Just as she was overtaking a convoy of lorries churning up so much water she could hardly see, the weather cut in, and she also caught a news bulletin about a hostage situation at Thornfield Reservoir. Unfortunately, the same gismo also cut the bulletin off halfway through the item. Annie jabbed at the search buttons. When she finally did get the right frequency, all she heard were the final words '. . . the hostage-taker has asked to talk to the detective in charge of the so-called Hobb's End skeleton case, Detective Chief Inspector Banks.'

Well, Annie thought, she would have to go back.

BANKS ARRIVED at Thornfield car park, put on his Wellington boots and hurried to the scene. Riddle hadn't been far wrong when he compared it to a Hollywood production. Though the patrol cars, Armed Response Vehicles and Technical Support Unit vans couldn't drive right to the rim of the reservoir because of the trees, some of them had forced their way through as far as they could, and long, thick wires and cables trailed the rest of the way. The local media people were there, too. The entire bowl of Hobb's End was floodlit. At the centre of it all, two small, pathetic figures were cruelly illuminated just beyond the fairy bridge.

Riddle stood by the phalanx of TV cameras clustered behind the police tape. Banks ignored him and went straight over to the hostage negotiator. He looked young. Banks guessed this was his first real-life situation. Officially, the local superintendent was in charge of the scene, but as a rule the negotiator called the shots.

'I'm DCI Banks,' he said.

'Sergeant Whitkirk,' said the negotiator.

'Let me go and talk to him.'

'You're not going down there,' Whitkirk said. 'Do your talking on this.' He held a loudhailer out. Banks didn't take it.

'No. You listen to me.' Banks pointed to the two figures. 'I don't know how many scenes like this you've handled successfully, but I know what this situation's all about and I think I've got a hell of a lot better chance than you or anyone else of making sure no one gets hurt. I know who he is and what he wants.'

'How can you know that? He hasn't communicated any demands.'

'Except to talk to me.'

'And our first rule is that we don't comply. He's a nutter and he's unpredictable. We can't give in to him, and you can't just walk into the situation. Maybe you're the one he really wants to kill.'

'I'll take my chances.'

Whitkirk thrust his chin out. 'No, you won't. I'm in charge of the scene here and you're not going in.'

'What do we do, then?'

'First we do all we can to turn an imprecise situation into a precise one.'

'Oh, stop quoting the textbook at me,' Banks said. 'Look, he's asked for me. He must have something to tell me, and there's only one way to find out. I think I can talk him out of doing any harm. Can't you give me a bit of leeway?'

Whitkirk chewed on his lip for a moment. 'Securing the scene's my responsibility,' he said.

'Let me go in.' Banks pointed over to the chief constable. 'Believe me, there's a bloke over there will give you a medal if I get shot.'

Whitkirk managed a thin smile. 'One condition,' he said. 'You wear a bulletproof vest.'

'All right.'

Whitkirk sent someone to pick up the vest from an Armed Response Vehicle, then he told the hostage-taker over his loud-hailer what he was planning.

'Send him in,' the man shouted back.

Kitted out with his bulletproof vest, Banks set off down the side of the reservoir. About halfway down, he slipped and went the rest of the distance on his backside. It reminded him that he had put on his best trousers. He had forgotten to phone Jenny and cancel.

He heard a curse behind him and turned to see Annie Cabbot

come sliding down after him. At the bottom, she flashed him a grin. 'Sorry. It was the only way I could give them the slip.'

'I take it you don't have a bulletproof vest?'

'No.'

'I could be gallant and give you mine, but we're a little too close to the scene now. Just stay back, behind me.'

They approached the fairy bridge and Banks told the man who he was. The man told them to stop at the far side. They faced one another over the bridge. Vivian Elmsley looked frightened but otherwise unhurt.

'This is DS Cabbot,' Banks said. 'She's been working on the case with me. Is it OK for her to be here?'

The man nodded. 'I know who she is,' he said. 'I saw her on television, then down here a week or so ago.'

'So it was you,' Annie said. 'What were you doing?'

'I've been here a lot at night. Thinking.'

'Why did you run?'

'I couldn't risk being caught, having to explain myself, before I'd finished what I had to do.'

Banks decided it was time to take charge. He held his hands up and gestured for Annie to do the same. Rain dripped down the back of his neck. 'We're not armed, Francis,' he said. 'We just want to talk. Let Ms Elmsley go.'

'So you know who I am?'

'Francis Henderson.'

'Clever. But my name's Stringer now. Frank Stringer.' So he had adopted his mother's maiden name. Strange. That told Banks something about the situation they were dealing with.

'Anyway,' Frank went on, 'I'm not ready to let anyone go yet. I want to hear it all first. I want to hear her confess to you, then I'll decide whether to kill her or not. It makes no odds to me.'

'OK, Frank. What do you want to hear?'

'She killed my mother. I want to hear her say so, and I want to know why.'

'She didn't kill anyone, Frank.'

'You're lying. You're trying to protect her.'

His grip tightened on Vivian. Banks caught her sudden intake of breath and saw the gun barrel pushed into the flesh under her ear.

'Listen to me, Frank,' he said. 'You want the truth, don't you? It didn't happen the way you think it did.'

'All those years,' Frank went on, as if he hadn't heard. 'Do you know he worshipped her, my father? He said she was a dreamer, a free spirit, a beautiful butterfly who just had to spread her wings and fly away. She always wanted to be one of those Hollywood actresses. But I hated her for leaving us. I hated her and I loved her. All my life dominated and blighted by a mother I never even knew. What do you think Mr Freud would make of that?'

'She *was* very young, Frank. When she got pregnant, she was frightened. She didn't know what to do. For some people, to run away seems like the only solution. She obviously wanted the child, *you*, to live. She didn't have an abortion. Did she keep in touch?'

He sniffed. 'A postcard every now and then, telling him she was doing fine. My dad took me up to Hobb's End to see her. It was the only time I . . . the only time I really remember seeing her, hearing her voice. She told me I was a fine-looking boy. I loved her then. She was a magical creature to me. Dazzling. So beautiful and so tender. But they argued. He couldn't help asking her to come back when he saw her, but she wouldn't. She told him she had a new life now and we should leave her alone if we wanted her to be happy.'

'What did your father do?'

'What she asked. He was devastated. We tried once more, when it was all over.' He turned so he was speaking into Vivian's ear. 'But this lying bitch here told us she had run away. All my life I believed that, believed my mother had run away and abandoned us for ever. Now I find out she was dead.'

'Let her go, Frank!' Banks shouted over a peal of thunder. 'She didn't know.'

'What do you mean, she didn't know? She must have known. Even if she didn't do the actual killing, she was involved.' Frank glared at Banks. His eyes were wild, his lank hair was plastered to his skull.

'You've got it all wrong, Frank. Vivian had nothing to do with your mother's death.' As he spoke, Banks noticed Vivian's eyes fill with curiosity, despite the gun at her neck. Annie stood beside him now. Banks's clothes stuck to his skin and rain stung his eyes.

'What do you mean?' Frank said.

'As far as she was concerned,' Banks said, 'your mother *had* gone away. She had spoken about running away often. Life was miserable for her. It was only natural for Gwen to assume that she'd go, just like she left you and your father in the first place.'

'No!'

Frank's grip tightened on Vivian's throat and she gasped. Banks felt his heart lurch. He held his hands out, palms towards Frank.

'OK, Frank,' he went on. 'Calm down. Please. Calm down and listen to me.'

They waited a moment, all silent but for the pattering of the rain and the storm disappearing into the distance.

Then Banks felt things relax. 'Matthew drove her away,' he went on. 'It was only natural for Gwen to assume that was what happened. Your mother's suitcase was gone. Her things were gone.'

Frank didn't say anything for at least a minute. Banks could see him processing information, trying to shore up his defences.

'If it wasn't her, who was it?' Frank said eventually.

Annie stepped forward. Frank turned to her and blinked the rain out of his eyes.

'His name was Edgar Konig,' Annie said. 'He ran the PX at Rowan Woods USAF Base, about a mile from here.'

'PX?' Vivian gasped.

'I don't believe you,' said Frank.

'It's true,' said Banks, picking up the thread. He realised that Annie didn't have the full story yet. 'Konig killed your mother. He also killed at least one other woman, down in East Anglia. There were others, too, in America.'

Frank shook his head slowly.

'Listen to me, Frank. Edgar Konig was attracted to your mother, but he had serious problems with women. He was always tongue-tied around them. He brought her presents, but even then she didn't offer herself to him. She went out with other men. He watched and waited. All the time the pressure was building up inside him.'

'How do you know it was him?'

'We found a collar button from an American airman's uniform. We think your mother must have torn it off as they struggled.'

Frank's grip round Vivian's throat had loosened a little.

'Edgar Konig went to Bridge Cottage to collect what he thought your mother owed him while her husband was at the pub. He'd been drinking and he thought he could overcome his inadequacies. She must have rejected him, maybe laughed at him, and the next thing he knew he'd killed her in a rage. Do you understand what I'm saying, Frank?'

'If that's how it happened, why did no one know about it?'

Slowly, Banks reached for his cigarettes and offered Frank one.

'Gave them up years back,' he said. 'Thanks, though.'

Banks lit up. Definite progress. Better not cock it up now.

'No one knew about it,' Banks went on, 'because Edgar Konig covered his tracks well.' He looked at Vivian Elmsley as he spoke. She averted her eyes. 'He buried the body in the outbuilding. Then he packed a few of her belongings in a suitcase to make it look as though she had run off. He even faked a note.'

Frank spoke in Vivian's ear. 'Is that right, what he's saying?'

Banks couldn't hear her, but he saw her mouth form the word 'Yes.'

'Frank,' Banks pressed on. 'The gun. I know you don't want to hurt anyone, but it's dangerous. It's easy to make a wrong move.'

Frank looked at the gun.

Banks stepped onto the fairy bridge and moved forward slowly. He knew there were probably two or three trained marksmen aiming in his direction, and the thought made his stomach churn. 'Give the gun to me, Frank.'

Frank released his grip on Vivian Elmsley's throat. She staggered aside and slipped down one of the muddy holes the SOCOs had dug in the Bridge Cottage floor. Annie ran to help her.

Frank handed the gun to Banks. 'What happened to him?' he asked. 'This Konig. Did he ever get caught?'

'I'll tell you all about that later, Frank,' said Banks, taking Frank by the elbow. 'Just for now, though, we're all a bit tired and wet. OK? I think we should go somewhere to dry off, don't you?'

Frank hung his head. Banks draped an arm across his shoulder. Several police officers had already come dashing and sliding down the embankment. Two of them grabbed Frank roughly and started handcuffing him.

'There's no need to be so rough with him,' said Banks.

'Leave this to us, sir,' said one of the officers.

Banks sighed and handed over the gun. They hustled Frank Stringer away. Banks turned to see Annie and the other policemen helping Vivian Elmsley to stumble over the fairy bridge.

'Thank you,' Vivian said. 'You saved my life.'

'I lied for you,' said Banks. 'I also sullied Gloria's loyalty to Matthew.'

She paled and whispered, 'I know. I appreciate what you did.'

'There was a chance, you know. If you'd come forward after you found Gloria dead, if you'd gone to the police . . .' Banks held his anger in check; this was neither the time nor the place for it. 'Ah, to hell with it. Too late now.'

Vivian bowed her head. 'Believe me, I know what I've done.'

Banks turned and slogged on through the mud to his car. All he wanted was a long hot bath and a large Laphroaig. And Annie.

She was already leaning against her car, arms folded.

'Are you all right?' Banks asked.

'I'm fine. Fine as anyone can be who's spent the last half-hour standing in the rain wondering if someone was going to get their head blown off. I respect what you did out there, by the way.'

'What do you mean?'

'You lied to get us all out of there alive.'

'It worked. What next?'

'Onward to St Ives. After I've stopped off for some dry clothes. I was already on my way when I heard. I couldn't just leave it.'

'Of course not. Thanks for being here.'

'You?'

'Home, I suppose.' Banks remembered dinner with Jenny. Too late now, but he could at least phone her and apologise.

Annie nodded. 'Look, I'll be gone for two weeks. Right now I'm still a bit mixed up about my feelings. Why don't you phone me when I get back? Maybe we can have that talk?'

'OK.'

She grinned at him crookedly. 'If there weren't so many policemen about I'd kiss you goodbye.' With that she opened the car door, got in and started the engine. Banks watched the red tail-lights disappear down the muddy track.

Epilogue

After a long, rainy winter and overdue repairs by Yorkshire Water, Thornfield Reservoir filled up again and Hobb's End once more disappeared. On July 27 of the year after the Gloria Shackleton murder had entered and left the public's imagination, Vivian Elmsley, in the midst of a national book tour, lay on a king-size bed in her Florida hotel room, alone with her memories, a bottle of gin, ice and tonic water, propped up with pillows, and watched the local news channel.

Tonight was the night, and after everything she had been through, Vivian desperately needed *some* sense of an ending.

Crowds gathered outside the gates of Starke Prison, about twenty-five miles away. One or two were quietly carrying placards that asked for an end to capital punishment, but by far the majority were chanting, 'Fry Konig! Fry Konig!' Vivian had been shocked when Banks told her that Gloria's murderer was not dead, but on death row in a Florida prison—a serial killer.

Vivian had visited Frank Stringer several times in jail and told him she would help him get back on his feet when he came out. It was the least she could do for Gloria's memory. In his turn, Frank had told Vivian how the re-emergence of Hobb's End had caused his obsession with the past to escalate. His father had been the first to recognise Gwen Shackleton as Vivian Elmsley on television, but Frank had confirmed it; he had memorised her eyes and her voice so many years ago. He couldn't explain why he had approached her at the bookshop. He meant no harm at first. Then the skeleton was discovered, and he knew she must have lied. He hated her after that; he telephoned to scare her, to make her suffer.

It was almost time. Edgar Konig, just turned seventy-six, was finally getting what he deserved.

Vivian felt a twinge of guilt when she realised that she *might* have helped put an end to his killing all those years ago. She had tried to rationalise it to herself so many times. Even if she had reported what happened, she told herself, they would have still probably arrested Matthew. What could she have told the police that would have pointed them towards Edgar Konig? It was all very well to say in retrospect that *she* could have stopped all those deaths, but it wasn't fair. Twenty-twenty hindsight. And who wouldn't, given the chance, go back and change *something*? Besides, Vivian told herself, she had acted only from the purest of motives: love for her brother.

And it was all over now. A cheer went up from the crowd outside the prison. Edgar Konig was dead.

Why was it that Vivian felt no relief, felt nothing but the stirrings of a bad headache? She closed her eyes. *All over.* She was so tired.

With her morbid imagination, Vivian saw Gloria run into the kitchen as she became frightened by PX's erratic behaviour, saw her pulling tins of tea and cocoa out of the cupboard, looking for the gun, shocked and scared to find that it wasn't there. Did she realise that Gwen must have taken it? *The gun.* Vivian was the one who had taken the gun, the one thing that *might* have saved Gloria's life.

Then, for all those terrible years, she had cared for Matthew, believing he was a murderer. Poor, gentle Matthew, who wouldn't harm a soul, who couldn't even kill himself. She had a vivid memory of the afternoon when she had come back from the shops and seen Matthew sitting with the gun in his mouth, trying to find the courage to pull the trigger. But he hadn't been able to do it. His eyes had pleaded with her, and she had walked over to him, tenderly wrapped her hand round his, kissed his forehead and pressed his finger on the trigger.

Outside Starke Prison the crowd was chanting. Vivian Elmsley let her tears flow freely for the first time in over fifty years.

PETER ROBINSON

Born and brought up in Yorkshire, author Peter Robinson already had a degree in English Literature from Leeds University under his belt when he chose to cross the Atlantic to continue his studies at the University of Windsor in Ontario.

Peter fell for Canada, and decided that he wanted to stay there, eventually making his home in Toronto, with his wife Sheila. His many successful detective novels, however, are set in the old country.

Part of the idea for *In a Dry Season* struck Peter Robinson in the late summer of 1995 when he was on holiday in England with his wife. They visited Thruscross Reservoir, near Otley in Yorkshire. The reservoir had dried up, and the remains of the old village of West End were on view for the first time since it had been flooded in 1967. They could see the foundations of houses, the ruined flax mill and a tiny packhorse bridge that had survived under water for almost thirty years. As a crime writer, Peter Robinson's first thought was: What an interesting place to discover a body!

Needless to say, the drought in Yorkshire did not last, but the author's fascination with his plot idea did. He created a fictional reservoir, borrowing the name Thornfield from Charlotte Brontë's *Jane Eyre*, and wove ingredients from the Second World War into the story. It was a period that interested Peter. Although he was not born until five years after the war ended, it cast its long shadow over his childhood, in the form of sweet rationing and bomb sites. For his hero, he already had the redoubtable Detective Chief Inspector Alan Banks, who has featured regularly in his novels since the first one, *Gallows View*, was published in 1987.